Also by Trae Dorn

The Mia Graves Series
The Witch and the Rose
Bloody Damn Rite
Shadowcasting

Comics and Graphic Novels
UnCONventional
The Chronicles of Crosarth
Peregrine Lake

Mia Graves Book Three

SHADOWCASTING

TRAE DORN

www.nerdandtie.com
www.traedorn.com

Copyright © 2024 by Trae Dorn

All rights reserved.

No part of this publication may be reproduced, distributed, or transmitted in any form or by any means, including photocopying, recording, or other electronic or mechanical methods, without the prior written permission of the publisher, except as permitted by U.S. copyright law.

This is a work of fiction. Unless otherwise indicated, all the names, characters, businesses, places, events and incidents in this book are either the product of the author's imagination or used in a fictitious manner. Any resemblance to actual persons, living or dead, or actual events is purely coincidental.

Cover designed by Getcovers

www.nerdandtie.com / www.traedorn.com

For Crysta.
Still and Always.

Prologue

The first fingers of dawn stretched their way through the gaps between barren trees giving an eerie glow to the snow covered ground. The wooded park along the Wabash River was one of the few places that felt truly wild in Parrish Mills, a scrap of nature nestled in a quaint college town surrounded by miles of level farmland.

Greg pulled his coat tightly around his slim frame as he made his way through the park, still baffled by the text that dragged him out into the cold this early. It would usually take a miracle to get Greg out of bed before noon, but this seemed more like the opposite of one. Greg was filled with dread, the pit in his stomach felt colder than the biting wind whipping through the morning air.

We need to talk about what you did. That was all it said, and then a location and time to meet. It was cryptic, it was bizarre, but it scared Greg just enough to get him there.

And Greg wasn't completely sure who sent it.

He had suspicions, of course. One name came to his mind in an instant. And it *had* to be her, right? She was the only one who knew. She was the only one who *could* know. But why would she send something like this? Lisa had made it very clear that they were done talking about this, and he knew she had just as much to lose as he did if any of it came out.

But who else could have sent it?

Greg couldn't just confront her. There was still a chance she wasn't the one who sent the message, that this was sent by someone else. If Greg was wrong, Lisa might retaliate and take drastic actions. If that happened, the consequences would be enormous.

There were too many possibilities. Maybe she'd told someone, maybe there was a witness he didn't know about, maybe someone had gotten into his phone...

Too many damned maybes.

Snap. Greg practically jumped out of his skin at the sound of a breaking twig. He looked down and saw the remnants of a stick under his boot and shook his head. He was tense. Too damned tense.

But it wasn't just him.

The air seemed to hold an energy that he couldn't define. It almost seemed heavy, like he was walking across the bottom of the ocean. He was off the path now, and the frozen ground turned into the sharp and fragile mud of the river bank, the ice cold river rushing before him.

"Greg," a voice whispered in his ear, and he whipped around to see no one there.

"Who's there? Who is that?" Greg demanded, clenching his hands into fists.

"We know what you did, Greg. We know who you are." The whispers seemed to be coming from all around him, but as far as he could tell no one was actually in the park with him. The dawn light seemed to fade, as though the sun had never risen. Greg tried to run, but found his feet attached firmly to the ground.

"What do you want from me!" Greg yelled, trying not to panic. The sky was almost black, and Greg swore he could see stars overhead again.

But these "stars" were wrong.

Rather than hold fixed positions in the sky, they began to swirl, cascading into spirals around Greg. Every moment growing closer and spinning faster.

"We don't want anything from you anymore, Greg," the voices whispered in his ear. "No one will ever want anything from you ever again. You will be forgotten."

The dancing stars suddenly became a blinding light, shining so bright that even when Greg closed his eyes it was like staring into the sun. The world felt like it was coming apart, the earth beneath him seemed to unravel, like a sweater being pulled apart by a loose thread. Greg tried to scream, but the air tasted like lavender and ice and no sound came from his mouth.

And then the fire came.

The fire seemed to erupt from within Greg's cells, and consumed him in an instant. It started like a gentle glow, like his body was harmonizing with the fabric of reality, but then the world turned sideways, and that warming glow erupted into an inferno, swarming Greg's body in an instant.

The only mercy was that it was so fast that Greg never felt a thing.

Chapter 1

"We have to stop him!" Mia yelled, running through the back alleys as fast as she could. Rain smashed against the ground, leaving the pavement slick with rivers of grime and trash. Her long, curly hair was matted against her face as she tried to keep her feet steady.

"Slow down, Mia!" Sarah replied, out of breath and not far behind. "You don't know what we're getting into!"

"We can't let Robbie do this!" Mia cried.

"But do you actually know *how* to stop him?" Sarah grunted.

"No, but I'll figure it out, damn it!" Mia said determinedly, her eyes flashing with a mix of fear and resolve. She skidded around a corner, nearly slipping on the wet ground, but managed to regain her balance just in time. The dimly lit alley seemed to go on forever, with shadows dancing menacingly in the corners.

Sarah caught up to her, her brow furrowed in concern. "Robbie's summoned demons before, Mia. He's a big boy, he can take care of himself."

"You don't understand," Mia said, pushing forward as quickly as she could. "This isn't a demon he's summoning. It's something else... I did some reading, and this shadow thing is way more dangerous. He's in way over his head with this thing."

As they rounded another corner, the sounds of the rain grew louder, echoing off the walls of the alleyway. Mia's heart pounded in her chest, a mix of fear for Robbie and frustration at his pure recklessness. She knew they had to intervene before it was too late.

"You can't just charge in there though," Sarah barked, trying desperately to keep up. "If it's as dangerous as you say, you could get hurt!"

Mia wasn't listening though. She was running as hard as she could, pushing forward with every ounce of strength she had. She didn't care that her legs burned, or that the rain water was soaked into every fiber of the clothes she wore. None of it mattered. None of it was important.

She needed to get to Robbie and stop him.

She didn't know why in the moment, but she knew things were about to go terribly wrong. That sense of dread and certainty built in her chest with such strength that she knew Robbie was in danger. If she could just get there in time, if she could just beg him to stop… maybe he'd live through this.

Maybe he'd survive *this time*.

Mia practically collided with a brick wall as she reached the end of the alley. A metal door to an unassuming apartment building sat in front of her, and she knew Robbie was somewhere on the other side. Mia reached for the handle.

"Mia stop," Sarah panted. "I don't… I don't want to relive this memory again."

Mia paused and turned around. Sarah seemed to almost flicker in the rain. Her chestnut brown hair got shorter, and her jacket seemed to be a bit more beaten up than it had been a moment ago.

"I don't… I don't know if this is your dream or if it's mine anymore, but whichever one of us is real right now…

we have to stop reliving this moment," Sarah cried. "I'm so tired of this. I'm so tired of reliving Robbie's death."

"I don't understand…" Mia started. "I can stop him. I can save him…"

"No, you can't," Sarah replied. "This already happened. This was five years ago. Robbie's gone, and no matter what you wanted to do, you can't change that."

Mia's breath caught in her throat as Sarah's words pierced through the fabric of reality. The world around her seemed to blur and distort, the rain frozen in midair like suspended crystals. She stared at Sarah, her eyes wide with a mix of disbelief and wrenching sorrow.

"I can't accept that," Mia whispered, her voice barely audible above the stillness that had enveloped them. "There has to be a way... I have to try."

Sarah's features softened, a glimmer of anguish flashing in her eyes as she reached out to touch Mia's arm. "I get it, Mia. I do. But we can't keep dwelling in the past, reliving our regrets and sorrows."

Mia stood there for a moment, the tears streaming down her face. "I just can't give up. I have to try."

"You know that if any of this was real, I wouldn't stop you from trying to save him," Sarah said quietly. "I'd be right behind you, like I was that night. I'd be telling you to keep going. To keep pushing."

Mia started to come out of the fog of the dream, and her memories began to find their way back to the surface. As she looked down, her arms were now covered in sigils and runes. She was starting to feel like herself again.

"My subconscious is really pulling out the greatest hits tonight, huh," Mia sighed.

"Still like fifty percent sure this is my dream and not yours, but yeah," Sarah said, brushing a lock of wet hair out of Mia's face. "Third time this week for this one."

"At least it's not the warehouse again," Mia sighed. "The warehouse is the worst."

"No disagreement there," Sarah shook her head. "Why can't we dream about that night where we snuck onto that rooftop with a bottle of wine and watched the sunrise? Why don't we ever get to dream about that."

"Or that time you took me out for my birthday after almost burning down our apartment trying to make me a cake," Mia smiled.

"Nope, instead we get another tragic night in Boston," Sarah replied. "God, at least one of us needs therapy."

"Probably both of us," Mia said, leaning against the wall. "But it's not like I could describe any of this without getting committed or something. 'I watched a good friend get consumed by a supernatural shadow thing' doesn't go over well."

"We could talk to each other?" Sarah suggested.

"Only one of us is real, and neither one of us is sure which," Mia laughed. "This is a dream. There's just one person having this conversation."

"I'm not saying it's a perfect idea, but it's better than nothing," Sarah shrugged. "I'm just trying to make sense of things."

"No, no… I get it—" Mia paused as the world seemed to pulse around her. It was as if reality itself shuddered, but it didn't feel like it was part of the dream. This felt *real*. "Did you… did you feel that?"

"Feel what?" Sarah asked, a puzzled expression on her face.

"Okay, it's settled. I'm the one who's dreaming—"

The world faded around Mia, as she groggily opened her eyes and came to in the real world.

****

Mia's studio apartment was a chaotic symphony of clutter and disarray, as though a tornado had swept through the small space and left only chaos in its wake. The single window, half-covered by a faded curtain, allowed a thin sliver of light to infiltrate the sanctuary of disorder. Mismatched furniture competed for space on the worn wooden floorboards that creaked beneath their weight; an ancient couch with frayed upholstery butted against a rickety bookshelf threatening to collapse under the burden of dusty tomes and arcane paraphernalia. Piles of unwashed laundry formed towering monuments to procrastination, and discarded dishes lay scattered like casualties on every available surface.

It was in this fortress of entropy that Mia Graves found herself entangled with Bobbi Crawford. Mia's eyes fluttered open, her dark brown irises slowly adjusting to the dim light. Her long curly black hair formed a tangled halo around her head, a testament to the previous night's passionate endeavors. She could feel the warmth of Bobbi's body pressed against hers, the rise and fall of her chest comforting and familiar in the early morning haze.

"Wha...?" Mia mumbled, her mind still thick with sleep. As she began to register her surroundings, the reality of the situation came flooding back. Bobbi had shown up at three in the morning, and Mia lacked the self control to stop her from coming in.

Bobbi was great, but she didn't require as much sleep as Mia did.

"Good morning," Bobbi murmured as she tightened her grip around Mia.

"Morning," Mia replied, her voice betraying her reluctance to leave the cocoon of warmth they had fashioned.

As she lay in her bed, thoughts and images from the previous night swirled around her mind, merging and melting together like the colors of an impressionist painting. The softness of the sheets whispered against her skin, and the warmth of the blankets embraced her like a safe cocoon, giving her a sense of security even as the edges of consciousness beckoned to her.

"I was surprised you came over last night," Mia said, running her hand along Bobbi's back. "I thought you and Blue were getting serious."

"Blue and I are done," Bobbi sighed. "We were just too different and it came to a head yesterday."

"Ah, that sucks, you really liked them," Mia said.

"Maybe I should just be like you and swear off relationships," Bobbi sighed. "Just settle for good friends and good sex." Bobbi's finger tracing one of the many tattoos that covered Mia's torso, back, legs and arms. Each one had a spell bound within its ink, and covered Mia's skin like a magical tapestry.

"I haven't sworn off relationships," Mia said, crinkling her nose. "I am open to love. I just haven't found it."

"Yeah, sure, I believe you," Bobbi smirked. "You're not emotionally closed off and secretly still hung up on your ex-girlfriend at all. Nope. Not even a factor."

"I am not—" Mia started.

"You talk about her in your sleep Mia," Bobbi smiled. "Like all the time. And, I get it. I'd be hung up on Sarah too. I *have* met her."

Mia pouted in mock protest, but it was hard to argue. If there was one thing she could trust Bobbi to do it was give Mia her unfiltered opinion.

"I have an idea," Bobbi murmured, her warm breath tickling Mia's chest. "What do you say to staying here all day? You can comfort me and I can make it worth your while."

Mia tried to clear her eyes, blinking away the sleep. She looked down at Bobbi nestled against her, her red hair a fiery contrast to the tangled mess of black curls that framed Mia's face.

"God, I'd love to, Bobbi," Mia whispered, her voice hoarse with the remnants of sleep. "But I can't. Have a store to run."

"Alright," Bobbi said, the corners of her mouth curling into a playful smile. She rolled onto her back, stretching languidly like a cat in a sunbeam. "But I'm demanding some Mia time later to make up for it. I am in dire need of distraction, and you owe me."

"Promise," Mia agreed, then glanced over at the clock on the bedside table. Her heart almost seemed to stop.

She had overslept.

Panic clawed its way up her throat, nearly choking her with the sudden urgency to get moving. There was so much to do, and now there was even less time to do it.

"Damn it!" Mia cursed under her breath, throwing off the warmth of the blankets and swinging her legs over the side of the bed.

"Everything okay?" Bobbi asked from under the rumpled sheets, a hint of concern in her voice.

"Fine," Mia replied tersely, already mentally calculating how much time she'd lost and what tasks she could afford to cut from her day. "I'm just incredibly late, I was supposed to meet up with Riley before work."

"Okay," Bobbi said softly, watching as Mia run around in a panic. "Say hi to her for me, I'm going to stay here in your bed and maybe eat your food so I don't have to go back to the dorms. It's way too cold out."

"That's fine, but the fridge is pretty empty," Mia breathed.

Mia's heart pounded as she started pulling clothes from what she hoped was the "clean-ish" pile. She grabbed out the first outfit she could find - a black A-frame tank top and form fitting pants that clung to her like a second skin. She tugged them on with haste, her movements frantic and unsteady.

Mia hated winter. The basic spells that kept her warm in the autumn and spring weren't powerful enough for the real cold, so she had to wear more layers. It meant her tattoos weren't anywhere near as accessible, and she was always so much more paranoid when she didn't have easy access to her spells.

Her boots went on next, knee-high and made from supple leather that had seen better days. She jammed her feet into them, forcing the zippers up with quick, jerky motions. The sigils tattooed across her body seemed to pulse with anticipation, feeding her growing anxiety.

Finally, she grabbed a long black coat that had been draped carelessly over a chair, shrugging it on without bothering to close it up. Mia took a deep breath, trying to calm her racing thoughts and focus on the task at hand.

"You're panicking like you're late, but you're literally the boss," Bobbi said, stretching luxuriously in the bed as she watched Mia scramble to get dressed. "You could always close the shop for the day and come back here after you see Riley."

"Pretty sure Zelda would get mad if I closed her store for the day, Bobbi," Mia retorted, rolling her eyes dramatically. She quickly brushed her teeth, pausing occasionally to glance around the room in search of her purse. Her mind raced, trying to remember where she had placed it amidst the chaos of her apartment. "Where the hell is that thing… have you seen my purse? The brown satchel?"

"Did you check under that pile of clothes on the floor?" Bobbi suggested, smirking as she pointed at six different piles at once. Mia shot her an exasperated glare.

"Very funny," Mia huffed, her cheeks flushing crimson. She couldn't help but laugh despite her mounting panic, appreciating Bobbi's attempts to lighten the mood. "Seriously though, have you seen my—"

"Purse? Yeah, it's right here," Bobbi interrupted, holding up the missing bag triumphantly. Mia's face broke into a grateful grin as she snatched it from Bobbi's hand, relief washing over her like a warm wave. "It was literally in the bed for reasons even I can't explain."

"Thank you," she breathed, pressing a quick kiss to Bobbi's cheek as she darted towards the door. "I owe you one. Gotta go now."

"Have fun! I'm going to eat all your food while watching videos of a Canadian Lesbian chopping wood on my phone," Bobbi smiled.

"Sounds productive and healthy," Mia smiled, grabbing a knit hat off of the couch and pulling it on. "Make sure you lock up when you get bored and finally remember I don't have a TV."

Mia's hurried exit from her apartment sent a shock of frigid air through her body, the bright winter morning sun doing little to counteract the chill. She squinted as snowflakes danced around her, swirling in the wind like playful spirits. The town of Parrish Mills was covered in a blanket of snow and ice, its streets lined with frost-kissed window panes and icicle-adorned rooftops.

With a sense of urgency pushing her forward, Mia raced down the snow-covered streets, her breath coming out in ragged puffs as she navigated the slippery sidewalks.

"Shit, shit, shit," Mia muttered under her breath, her heart pounding in her chest. She could practically hear the tick-tock of time slipping away from her. If Riley was late for work because she waited for Mia at the coffee shop Mia wouldn't forgive herself. It wasn't like her to oversleep, but last night's passionate encounter with Bobbi had left her spent and drained.

Bobbi was great, but she was young and had way more energy than Mia did.

The coffee shop finally came into view, a shining beacon of warmth amidst the icy landscape. Relief washed over Mia as she reached for the door handle, pausing briefly before stepping inside.

As soon as Mia crossed the threshold, the enticing aroma of freshly brewed coffee enveloped her, awakening her senses and driving away the last remnants of sleep. The cozy interior of the coffee shop was a stark contrast to the frigid world outside, with its mismatched chairs, worn wooden tables, and walls covered with the eclectic creations of local artists.

"Hey!" Riley called out from their usual booth by the window, her bright smile illuminating the cozy space. She raised her hand in greeting, her long blonde hair cascading over her shoulders as she leaned back, nursing a steaming cup of coffee.

"Riley!" Mia exclaimed, her voice tinged with relief and excitement. A surge of affection swelled within her as she strode towards the booth, feeling at home in Riley's presence — a rare reprieve from the storm of emotions brewing inside her.

"Finally," Riley teased, her eyes twinkling with amusement. "I thought I'd have to send a search party for you."

"Sorry," Mia panted, sliding into the booth opposite her best friend, her cheeks flushed from the cold and her hurried journey. "Overslept."

"Again?" Riley arched a brow, taking a slow sip of her coffee. "You really need to invest in a better alarm clock, Mia."

"Or maybe just learn to say 'no' to Bobbi once in a while," Mia muttered, shrugging off her winter coat and folding it over the edge of the table. She caught the knowing smirk on Riley's face and rolled her eyes. "How was your night?"

"Same old, same old," Riley sighed, stirring her coffee absentmindedly. "I've been trying to get this paper into a publishable state, but I don't know. I think I need a brain break. Want to go out and get absolutely plastered tonight?"

"I think I can make time in my busy schedule," Mia grinned. "You thinking the Siren?"

"Sounds like a plan." Riley's smile widened, her eyes warm and inviting. "Then I can crash on your couch or something instead of trying to make it home."

"Might want to call a cab," Mia sighed. "Bobbi broke up with Blue, so I'm pretty sure she's coming back over again. I think I'm being used for... emotional comfort?"

"Oh, you'll be 'comfortable' all right," Riley laughed.

"Hold that thought, we're short on time and I need coffee," Mia smiled, heading to the counter. The dark haired barista greeted Mia with a smile. After a quick exchange of banter Mia handed over a sum of money that amounted to more than what a coffee should really cost in a just world.

While waiting for her order to get made, Mia took a moment to collect herself, her thoughts still racing a mile a minute. She couldn't shake the feeling that something was off, an uneasiness that gnawed at her gut. Was it just the lingering effects of her recurring dream? Or was it something more sinister?

Dreams involving Sarah had the annoying tendency to *mean something* most of the time.

The barista returned quickly with Mia's coffee, and with her hot beverage in hand she made her way back to Riley.

"Again, I'm sorry I'm so late," Mia sighed. "I thought that by moving the store opening an hour later I'd somehow start getting it together in the mornings."

"Your optimism is adorable," Riley laughed. "I'm pretty sure that you're destined to wake up thirty minutes after whatever alarm you set no matter what time it is."

"God, I don't even have time to sit down, do I," Mia said, shaking her head.

"You do not," Riley said, standing up. "I need to get going or I'm going to be late to teach my nine o'clock..."

"I'll walk with you back to campus then?" Mia said shrugging. "We can cut through Riverside Park. It'll save you five minutes or so."

"Ugh, really?" Riley scrunched her nose up at the thought. "The company is welcome, but that park creeps me out. You and Sarah found that vampire there…"

"That very dead vampire, I will remind you. Also it's daytime, so not really a risk," Mia smirked, putting her coffee cup in its paper sleeve and shrugging back on her coat. "But yeah. It'll get you to your class with time to spare."

"Fine," Riley acquiesced. "But if I see some unspeakable horror along the way, you owe me a coke."

The two women made their way outside, the cold air nipping at their faces as they found their way to the park that wrapped itself around the northern riverbank. Snow crunched beneath their boots, and the water flowed sluggishly, half-frozen and seemingly hesitant to embrace its icy fate.

"Damn, it's freezing," Mia muttered, taking a slow sip of her drink. The rich taste of the coffee mixed with a hint of cinnamon spread across her tongue, warming her insides.

"Welcome to winter in Parrish Mills," Riley quipped, her voice laced with a trace of smugness. She grinned at her friend before taking a sip of her own coffee, savoring the smooth blend of flavors. "This is only your second one, and they get way worse than this. Winter gets real here."

"We had winter in Boston, I've lived with 'real winter' my whole life," Mia said shaking her head. "The California girl does not get to play all high and mighty on this one."

"You know I went to grad school in Chicago, I've been in the Midwest for a while," Riley laughed. "Tell me why on Earth is the great Mia Graves so whiny about the cold if she's so used to it then?"

"Being used to something doesn't necessarily make you stop hating it," Mia replied. "Bobbi asked me to stay in bed with her today, and I think I'm definitely regretting not taking her up on it now."

The sound of their footsteps provided an oddly soothing rhythm, punctuating their conversation as they continued their walk deeper into the wooded park. Despite the beauty of the surrounding landscape, adorned with glittering ice and pristine white snow, Mia couldn't shake the ominous feeling gnawing at the edge of her consciousness.

"Riles, do you ever get the sense that things are just...too quiet?" Mia asked, her voice barely audible above the wind's whispers.

"Quiet? You mean like when we're walking in the woods by a half-frozen river in the dead of winter?"

"Very funny," Mia retorted, rolling her eyes. "I mean more like an eerie silence, a stillness that doesn't feel quite right."

Riley furrowed her brow, her expression growing serious. "Now that you mention it, something does kind of feel off right now. Like the air's got a weight to it? Almost like it's heavy."

As they walked, Mia felt the hair on the back of her neck stand up. Her heartbeat quickened, each thud echoing loudly in her ears, drowning out all other sounds. The overcast sky overhead seemed to close in on them, like there was an ominous shadow over the riverbank.

"Riles, stop," Mia said abruptly, her voice tense and urgent. "Something's not right here."

"Wha--" Riley began, but Mia cut her off with a firm grip on her arm, her dark eyes scanning their surroundings, searching for the source of her unease.

"Stay close to me. I don't know what it is, but we need to be careful." Mia's breaths were shallow, her body coiled and ready for action.

"I don't like that look on your face," Riley sighed. "It's never good when you have that look on your face."

Chapter 2

Riley steadied herself in the cold. Mia was usually right about this kind of thing, but Riley knew that she'd overreacted once or twice before. She really, really hoped it was one of those times.

"Are you sure you're not worrying over nothing?" Riley asked, the frigid wind off the river carrying with it a bone-deep chill. "Because I think you might be worrying over nothing."

"Something's just... *off*, Riley. I haven't been able to shake this feeling all morning, and it's gotten worse the further we go," Mia murmured, her voice barely above a whisper. Her eyes scanned the woods where the skeletal fingers of bare trees clawed at the brooding sky. Mia seemed to shiver, but Riley knew it wasn't from the cold.

"Okay, what do you mean by off?" Riley asked, shifting her weight from one foot to the other, trying to keep the blood flowing. The wind shifted directions abruptly, and the odor hit her like a semi truck. The smell was pungent, like burnt hair mixed with rotten eggs. The air itself felt almost violent to inhale, and it clawed its way into Riley's sinuses. This was worse than the smell of death. This was like the smell of an unmaking.

"God Mia, do you smell that?"

"Smell what?" Mia's brow furrowed, but then it hit her too, and she recoiled trying not to gag. Mia's hand went to the tattoo on the back of her neck instinctively, and Riley felt her stomach drop as she realized the exact words Mia was going to say before she said them. "We need to figure out what that is."

"Ugh, I'd really like to go the opposite direction. It's like a skunk bathed in sulfur," Riley complained, covering her nose with the sleeve of her jacket. "God, I want to scrub my nose out with bleach right now."

Mia nodded, her body clearly filled with tension. "We need to find out where it's coming from." Her voice was firm, commanding, leaving no room for argument. She started walking towards the river.

"I know that look on your face, I don't like it when you have that look on your face," Riley said, following behind Mia. "That look literally never turns out well."

The stench intensified as they moved further off the path, clawing at their sinuses. Riley tried not to gag.

"God, it's like the air has teeth," Riley muttered. She hesitated, her steps faltering as they neared the foul miasma's source.

"Stay close," Mia instructed. It had been a milder winter, and river's lazy currents whispered to their right, indifferent to the macabre discovery awaiting them.

They rounded a patch of barren trees, and the solid ground beneath their feet gave way to the muddy banks of the river. Riley audibly gasped as they came upon the gruesome scene: a charred corpse sprawled on the winter morning snow.

"God damn it..." Riley's words caught in her throat. She had seen a lot in the last year and a half, but this was beyond any of it so far. "What kind of person would do this to someone?"

"Let's hope it was a person," Mia said quietly, her gaze locked onto the blackened figure. The body, or what was left of it, lay contorted, its features melted away by intense heat. It was a tableau of horror, painted in ash and frozen earth.

"I would like to stop finding dead bodies with you, I know this is only the second time, but two is two too many," Riley whispered.

"Three if you count Lila's bones, but I'm one hundred percent there with you on that," Mia replied. "Look for stuff that's out of place, but don't touch anything." Mia crouched beside the remains, her eyes skimming the area for clues invisible to those who didn't know to look for the occult.

"Yeah, I'm obviously not going to touch anything," Riley shook her head. "Why on earth would I want to touch any of this?"

Riley watched Mia grab the back of her neck with one hand again, and her breath seemed to catch in her throat.

"It's like standing at the edge of a chasm," Mia whispered, the words slipping out as her fingers grazed her neck. "It's like someone tore open the fabric of reality right here. This reeks of dark and potent energy. This was magic, Riley. Really powerful magic."

"So it was a spell," Riley said quietly. "Some witch just went and fried someone in the park last night?"

"A witch, a sorcerer, a ceremonial magician... whatever label they use, yeah." The ominous tone of Mia's voice sent a shiver down Riley's spine. "Whoever did this wielded power that is way outside the norm. The amount of energy that did this shouldn't even be possible without blowing up half a city block."

The math on that didn't quite add up for Riley. In the almost year and a half she'd been friends with Mia, she'd seen some wild things — and none of this looked like it would be that hard to pull off. Frankly, it was a charred body. A lighter and some gas would do the same thing.

"I don't really follow. It's just fire, I've seen you pull fire out of the air plenty," Riley replied. "I've had to talk you out of doing it in public when you were drunk, even."

"This guy wasn't burned with fire. For this kind of energy to still be sitting in the air, it means he was burned with raw, pure magical energy. Like reality folding stuff," Mia said, looking back at Riley. "This is insane – who would use this kind of spell just to kill one guy? It's like using a nuclear bomb to light a match."

"So that's not good," Riley said. "How would someone do that?"

"There are only a few methods that I can think of, and they have consequences," Mia replied. "And those consequences are really, really bad."

"As in 'more people might die' bad?" Riley asked.

"Yeah, as in 'more people will *definitely* die' bad," Mia answered.

The words hung heavy in the air, laden with implications that neither of them wanted to acknowledge.

A glint caught Riley's eye, something half-buried among the ashes. She reached down, retrieving a charred wallet, its edges still warm. "Hey, got something," she announced, flipping it open to reveal an ID, singed but legible. "Greg Van Buren..."

"What happened to not touching anything, Riley," Mia said, rolling her eyes. "Like, I literally just said not to touch stuff."

"Yeah yeah yeah, whatever you say, Rizolli," Riley said dismissively. Looking at the ID longer, she paused, her voice dropping lower. "Oh god, I know this guy, Mia. He was a student in one of my classes last semester. He barely passed, but sweet kid."

"There's something else," Mia said quietly. A swirl of lines and curves etched into the frozen earth, seemed to pulse with a life of its own under the Mia's scrutiny.

"What is that?" Riley asked, squatting down next to Mia.

"A sigil. It looks familiar, but I can't quite place it," Mia murmured, tracing the outline with a finger, even Riley could feel the echo of magic that had once saturated the ground. "Whoever did this did it right here in the park, in person, up close. That's not easy. Something like that takes preparation. This was planned."

"Great, premeditated magical murder," Riley sighed. She wasn't sure if the cold she felt right now was from the actual winter air or from the implications.

"Which means they're dangerous, and full of rage. I can practically taste it. The magical energy here is just echoes of pure anger," Mia said, her voice a low growl. "This is someone on a vendetta. Someone looking for revenge maybe."

"And angry people don't usually care about collateral damage," Riley added, her mind already sifting through the possibilities.

"No, no they don't," Mia agreed, standing up. Her shadow stretched long over the grisly scene. The morning air felt charged, the fabric of reality seemed thinner where the murder had occurred, and it whispered of unseen dangers lurking just beyond perception.

"Greg must've crossed paths with someone very powerful—or pissed off the wrong coven." Mia paced, the restlessness in her veins morphing into a fierce resolve. "We need to do something about this."

"Okay, so where do we start?" Riley asked, her breath forming clouds in the chill air. "I mean, besides the obvious 'call the cops and tell them we found a body' part."

"First, I'm going to try and find out more about this symbol." Mia knelt again, her fingers hovering above the sigil, tracing its edges in the air as if she could divine its secrets through proximity alone. "I'll have to hit the books. There has to be a record of this somewhere. This thing looks like ceremonial magic, and those guys wrote literally everything down. Sometimes they wrote it in stupid code, but still."

"Great, a needle in a haystack. My favorite kind of search," Riley quipped, though her jest didn't quite mask the nerves underneath.

"More like a needle in a stack of needles buried under a needle factory," Mia corrected, half-smiling despite the grimness of their task. With one final, piercing look at the charred husk that was once Greg Van Buren, she turned on her heel, her heart pumping a cocktail of adrenaline and dread through her veins.

"Come on," she urged Riley, her voice barely above a whisper, as if speaking too loudly would summon the perpetrator from the shadows.

Riley nodded, her fingers trembling as she retrieved her phone from the pocket of her pantsuit. "Why yes Mia, I'll be the one to call it in to the cops, thank you for asking me to," she said sarcastically, dialing with stiff fingers, her breath misting in the frigid air. Riley stayed there for a few minutes, relaying the information to the dispatcher. The distant sound of sirens would soon follow, an alarming wail to break the quiet Parrish Mills morning.

As they hurried back toward the safety of civilization, the soles of their shoes crunched over the frost touched earth, keeping tempo with their racing thoughts. Riley mind was a tempest, each gust of wind whipping up new questions, scenarios, and fears. What sort of person could wield magic with so much force that it would freak out Mia? And why this random kid?

"Whoever did this... They're playing with fire—literally." Riley quipped, trying to distract herself from what they had just witnessed.

"More like playing with folding reality, but you get burned either way," Mia replied, her words laced with anger and a hint of foreboding sarcasm.

"Oh, so reality just might shatter and we all die in the fall out," Riley added grimly. "No biggie."

"Exactly. We have to stop them before this happens again," Mia nodded. "What do you remember about Greg?"

"Not a ton, pretty typical frat guy, a little bro-y," Riley shook her head. "But a nice kid, not exactly the type you expect to get wrapped up into the mystical, y'know?"

"That might make this harder," Mia said quietly. "If it turns out he was selected as a random victim, it's going to be difficult figuring out who did it."

"Oh god, I don't even want to consider that," Riley replied.

The two stepped out of the park and onto the busy downtown street. As life filled the winter morning around them, it was hard to imagine that the death and darkness they'd stumbled across just lay just out of sight.

"I'm sorry that you're probably late for your class now," Mia said, sighing. "Stop by the store when you're done for the day, and we can start figuring this out."

"Sounds like a plan," Riley responded. "And Mia?"
"Yeah?"
"You owe me a fucking coke."

Chapter 3

The last tendrils of twilight crept through the stained-glass windows of Markov Books, casting a kaleidoscope of shadows across the stacks of tarot decks and mass produced witchcraft books. Mia pulled the cash drawer from the register, and began to count it down. The day had gone quickly, and beyond the morning's grisly events had otherwise passed uneventfully.

"Alexis, could you turn off the open sign and sweep the aisles," Mia called out, manually flipping through the dollar bills. She watched the young woman, Alexis Biedermann, turn off the neon sign that hung on the front window, fingers trembling slightly as she found the switch. The girl's shyness was nearly palpable, each gesture measured, as if she was afraid she might scare anyone around her with a sudden movement — including herself. Mia had hired her two months ago, and the girl still seemed to be a bundle of nerves when she was in the store.

"Y-Yes ma'am," Alexis stammered, her voice barely rising above a whisper, eyes darting around the room.

"Thanks, Alexis. You did good work today," Mia said, not missing the faintest flicker of pride in the girl's gaze before it was quickly doused by her habitual reserve.

The chime above the door interrupted the hush, heralding the arrival of Riley Whittaker, whose sharp features were momentarily softened by the evening light. "Heyo, ready to dig into this bullshit?" Riley asked, gesturing to a folder tucked under her arm.

"Ready as I'll ever be," Mia replied. "Let's take this back into my office."

Riley nodded, her blonde hair catching the remnants of light as she brushed past a display of crystal balls and rose quartz. "After you."

"Alexis, if you could lock the door I'd appreciate it," Mia said, picking up the cash drawer and coming out from behind the counter.

Riley and Mia walked back to a small office tucked in the back of the shop leaving Alexis tp continue to close up the store. Mia settled into a well used leather desk chair held together largely by duct tape and hope, and opened her work laptop.

"Find anything worthwhile?" Mia asked while logging into her machine, her ears tuned to the sound of Riley rifling through her folder. "I think I'd take anything at this point."

"Honestly I'm not sure, and half of what I've done here one hundred percent violates FERPA," Riley muttered, sitting on the edge of Mia's desk and slapping a sheaf of papers down. "Greg's student records are a bit of a mess. Kid was all over the place. Literally declared five majors in two years."

"College kid has no idea what he wants to do with his life, not a huge shock," Mia shrugged. "Standard middle-class white boy early life paralysis."

"Did you find anything looking through his social media?" Riley asked.

"I'm not sure," Mia said, leaning back in her chair. "Most of his posts look like the frat boy activity you'd expect. Dumb kids doing dumb kid stuff."

"Did you notice who his dad is?" Riley replied, pointing at one of the sheets she'd brought. "Greg Van Buren is the son of Thomas Van Buren."

"I feel like you think I should know who that is," Mia said, raising an eyebrow.

"The state senator?" Riley said, looking at Mia like she was from the moon. "You've lived in this town for like a year and a half and you don't know who your state senator is? You're registered to vote, aren't you?"

"I mean, I keep meaning to..." Mia said quietly. "I try to keep my name off of government records as much as I—"

"Oh my god, when we're done with this, we are registering you to vote," Riley interrupted. "It's just filling out a form on a website in Indiana. Voting is *important*. You're a queer woman in a red state, you need to-"

"Okay, okay!" Mia said, throwing her hands up in the air in surrender. "I'll do it. Can we stick with the magical murder though? Yikes."

"Fine, fine. Back to the murder," Riley said, gesturing to the stack of papers. "The main problem I'm having is trying to figure out how Greg ended up on the receiving end of magical murder. Everything looks so ordinary here."

"Same," Mia replied, shaking her head. "Like I don't want to stereotype, but I don't see anyone in any of these posts who looks like an obvious witch?"

"I mean, they're all guys, so of course not?" Riley said with a shrug.

"Witch is a gender neutral term, Riles," Mia said shaking her head. "Mike, who used to work here? Probably one of the best herbal witches I've ever met."

"Didn't you describe Mike as the most boring man who's ever existed?" Riley asked. "Like how did *he* 'look like a witch?'"

"Being a witch doesn't automatically make you *not boring*, and when you know what you're looking for, it's obvious," Mia said. "There's more than one type, and Mike fits into one of them. He's like the khaki pants version at least."

"So, okay, we don't think Greg was doing witchcraft himself, and it's no one in his current circle," Riley continued. "So we're assuming he wronged someone who he's not currently friends with?"

"I think that's gotta be it," Mia said, clicking through Greg's social media feed. "I don't see anything here that..."

Mia stopped talking as she pulled up another picture. It was an older photo of Greg with a dark haired young woman. A young woman that Mia recognized.

"I know this girl," Mia said, looking closely at the photo.

Riley leaned in as Mia turned the laptop towards her. In the heart of a boisterous group, Greg stood with his arm wrapped around a dark-haired girl whose eyes held a storm that belied her smile.

"It's tagged Lisa Farris," Riley murmured.

"Yeah, for like six months she was in here almost every week," Mia said. "Then like in November she stopped coming in? I assumed she just moved on like a lot of folks do."

"Do we think she might be our witch?" Riley asked.

"Definitely worth looking into," Mia nodded. "She spent a lot of time looking at sigil work. Asked about my tattoos on more than one occasion."

"Does that tell us anything?" Riley asked.

"Not sure, but I know she developed her own," Mia answered. "Had it stitched onto her bag. I think she--"

"Um, Mia?" Alexis's voice cracked through the open door, interrupting their conversation.

"Hey, Alexis." Mia stopped what she was doing to look up at the young woman. "What's up?"

Alexis fidgeted with the strap of her messenger bag, eyes darting from Mia to Riley and back again. "I'm going to head out, if that's okay? It's getting late."

"Of course," Mia replied, finally turning with a reassuring smile that didn't quite reach her worried eyes. "Take the back door out, so I don't have to relock the front?"

"Sure thing, Mia." Alexis offered a nod, then hesitated, as if on the verge of speaking further. But the moment passed, and she slipped away, leaving behind the echo of her soft footfalls retreating into the night.

"That girl looks like she's scared of her own reflection," Riley observed, staring at the space that Alexis had just occupied.

"Yeah, she is certainly that," Mia conceded. "But she's reliable. And I'll take reliable over brave any day of the week."

With a sigh, Mia reached for the bottom drawer of her desk. The sound of wood scraping against wood heralded the reveal of a well-worn bottle of whiskey, its golden contents catching the light like liquid amber. She twisted off the cap, the scent of aged spirits filling the room, mingling with the musk of old leather and ink.

"So if we're going to cyberstalk a college girl, I'm going to need to be less sober than this," Mia declared, pouring two generous measures into mismatched glasses. She slid one across the desk to Riley, who accepted it with a solemn nod.

"Here's to trying to do this without being creepy." Riley raised her glass slightly.

"Oh god I hope that's possible," Mia added wryly, downing her drink in one fluid motion. The burn of the whiskey was a welcome flare in the dimness.

"Hey, it's only creepy if she turns out to be a bystander," Riley replied.

"I don't know if I hope she is one, or if I hope she's not," Mia said settling into her chair.

"It looks like she and Greg used to be together," Riley said, clicking through images on Mia's computer. "Bad breakup maybe? Embittered hormonal kid uses dark magic on her ex?"

"Wouldn't be the first time, though ripping apart reality goes a bit further than I'd expect." Mia turned the computer back to herself, fingers dancing across the keys as she called up Lisa's social media profiles. Images flickered past — smiles, parties, moments captured in digital amber — each one a potential clue or a red herring.

"Tomorrow, we dig deeper into her life," Mia said, her voice laced with a steel that matched the resolve in her heart. "I also might swing by Zelda's, and get her take on things."

"I still don't buy that Zelda Markov is actually a person," Riley smirked. "I'm convinced you've made her up, and that the store is actually owned by some corporate conglomerate out of, like, Ohio or something."

"I can never tell if you're doing a bit or not with this whole 'Zelda isn't real' schtick," Mia laughed.

"One day you'll puzzle it out," Riley said with a laugh. "But tonight, let's just get drunk instead."

Chapter 4

Mia barged through the door of Robbie's apartment. She knew this was a dream of a memory. She knew she couldn't stop him. She knew there was nothing she could do to change what happened or save her friend.

But a part of her had to keep trying.

"Robbie, stop!" Mia yelled, reciting the words she knew would do nothing. "This thing will kill you!"

Robbie looked up at her as he knelt in the center of the apartment's worn carpet. A series of sigils were crudely scrawled into the carpet around him in sharpie, and lit candles marked the borders of a circle around him.

"Mia, relax, I know what I'm doing," Robbie smirked, overconfident as always. "I'm just going to summon it to figure out how it works. I've got more than enough protective sigils primed to keep it from hurting me."

Sarah came through the door behind Mia, trying her best to keep up. She looked both sad and irritated. Mia didn't remember Sarah looking like this that night. Mostly she remembered Sarah looking scared.

"God damn it Mia, just stop?" Sarah said, supporting herself on the doorframe as she caught her breath. "It's just going to turn out the same way. It does every time."

"I don't... I can't accept that..." Mia stammered. Robbie kept moving, seemingly unable to hear either of them.

"It's just going to be the same," Sarah shook her head. "You'll try to convince Robbie that this shadow thing is too dangerous and that he can't control it, Robbie ignores you and performs the ritual anyway — saying that once he masters these creatures he can achieve anything. Then *this* happens."

Mia turned back to Robbie. Time seemed to have jumped forward, and Robbie now stood, head back, arms out, and tendrils of darkness writhing and circling around his body.

"No…" Mia said quietly, dropping to her knees. "I could have…"

"You have to let it go, Mia. It's not your fault. It was never your fault," Sarah said, kneeling down and placing her hand on Mia's back. "I know you feel like you have to try, but you can't save people who don't *want* you to save them. And you especially can't save people who have been dead and gone for five years. You have to get past this."

"I thought I *was* past this," Mia said barely above a whisper. "Why am I dreaming this? Why do I keep coming back to this *now*?"

"I don't know," Sarah replied. "I think the bigger question is why am *I* dreaming this now?"

****

Mia's old, rusty Ford Ranger roared and banged with a cacophony of protest as she maneuvered her way through the narrow snow covered streets towards the outskirts of Parrish Mills. Mia didn't like to admit that she needed advice sometimes, but with the kind of energy she'd felt around Greg's body, she definitely needed a second opinion.

And there was only one witch in this small town town more experience than Mia Graves.

Zelda owned the store Mia managed, but steadfastly avoided it most of the time. In the approximate year and a half that Mia had worked for Zelda, Mia could count the number of times Zelda had actually set foot in the store on two hands. Frankly, since Mia had been promoted to manager, Zelda had only been in the place once.

But Mia needed Zelda's help, and if Zelda wasn't going to come to her, she was going to come to Zelda.

Mia pulled her truck into Zelda's driveway and put it into park. The house was just an ordinary ranch nestled in the shadows of barren winter trees and well maintained hedges. Just another one of many on the block. No passerby would suspect that the extraordinary might live inside its walls, it just wasn't that sort of place. The home was well maintained, but small. Mia had been here once before in the spring, and the snow was hiding a well appointed garden that would wake up in a few months.

Zelda was the kind of person who didn't need her home to stand out. She could do that all by herself.

Mia's knuckles rapped against the door, and she waited with nervous anticipation. It took a few moments longer than Mia expected before the door creaked open, but it soon revealed the enigmatic figure of Zelda Markov.

"Ah, Mia," Zelda greeted, her voice like velvet laced with steel. She was in her sixties, and a full head shorter than Mia. Dressed in a black silk robe, Zelda's white hair cascaded down her back, a waterfall of moonlight contrasting with the darkness behind her. "Bit of an awkward moment to show up, but with this cold you should really come in before you catch your death out there."

Mia stepped into the dimly lit room, the scent of incense and cedar enveloping her as she crossed the threshold. Zelda's home was full of knick-knacks and chaos, a veritable ode to eclecticism.

"Thanks, Zelda," Mia replied, her voice slightly shaky, betraying her nerves. "I... need your advice."

"I do wish you'd call first before coming over," Zelda's gaze lingered on Mia's face for a moment, studying the shadows that danced in her dark brown eyes. "I do have a busy life outside of handing out random sage advice, but with that expression on your face I assume this is urgent?"

"So you know how that college student was found dead by the river yesterday?" Mia asked carefully. "In the park on the edge of downtown?"

"Oh of course dear, the state senator's kid," Zelda nodded. "It's been all over the news. A bit hard for me to miss."

"It was magic," Mia said quietly. "And not just any kind of magic. Whoever killed him used something powerful. Something dangerous."

Zelda paused for a moment thoughtfully. "How do you know?" she asked thoughtfully. "From what they said on the news, he was burned, and fire from a spell doesn't leave much of a signature or trace behind. What little it would leave isn't something that could last all that long either."

"My friend Riley and I are the ones who found the body," Mia explained. "And he wasn't burned with fire. It was raw, unfiltered magic. It was like the fabric of reality was vibrating with it around the body."

Zelda's smile faded. This was the first time Mia had ever seen even a flicker of fear in the older woman's eyes.

"If anyone other than you told me that, I probably wouldn't believe them," Zelda said quietly. "You're one hundred percent sure about that?"

"It was the kind of thing I've rarely seen before," Mia replied. "It was like reality was almost torn apart.

Channeling that kind of energy should be impossible for a witch without destroying themself. The only other time I saw something with this much of a post-ritual metaphysical impact it left three dead and a half a dozen other witches completely burnt out, never able to touch magic again. Greg was the only corpse, and he's wasn't a magic user from what I could tell"

"If they were doing things the conventional way, sure," Zelda said, walking to a bookcase. "But there are techniques that can avoid those limits. Dangerous ones, with consequences that are, pardon my language, pretty fucking bad."

"That's the kind of thing I was afraid of," Mia replied. "I just didn't want to believe it."

"This kind of magic is a fickle beast," Zelda said, her voice low and ominous. "Just because the typical consequences of using this kind of power have been subverted, doesn't mean there are none. If anything, they may end up becoming so much worse."

"Worse than dying?" Mia asked tentatively.

"Depends on how you die," Zelda replied. "And what's left of your soul afterwards."

A shiver ran down Mia's spine, as if the echoes of her own past were a driving wind.

"The people wielding this energy are a danger," Zelda said, picking up a book from the shelf. "Not just to other people, but also to themselves. What do you know about 'true shadows?"

At the mention of a true shadow, Mia's breath caught in her throat, her pulse quickening with a mixture of dread and fascination. Maybe her dreams this week hadn't been as random as she thought.

"I saw one once, and that was more than enough for me," Mia said. "Mostly that it's incredibly hard to get their attention, but if you do... you're can't escape it. Lost a good friend to one after he purposefully summoned one mistakenly thinking he could control it."

"That's more than most witches know," Zelda said, handing a book to Mia. It was an old leather bound volume with aged and damaged pages. "And frankly, usually they don't need to. Most of our people just know not to summon one on purpose, and would be dead long before they pulled in the kind of power that could draw a true shadow in on its own volition."

"And that's the kind of magic I sensed," Mia said, paging through the book. "Which means..."

"Which means that a true shadow may be on its way," Zelda continued. "They just... consume. They're the absence of energy, the absence of life. You can't fight them, you can't stop them. You avoid them, and do your best not to draw their attention."

"Bad news all around," Mia sighed, shaking her head. Only about half of what Zelda was telling her was new information, but it was confirming her worst fears.

"Once a shadow starts hunting there's very little to stop it," Zelda said, running her hand through her long white hair. "If its found and touched its prey, the only way to survive is by cutting them off from all magic. Severing the shadow's target from the flow of the universe."

Mia nodded solemnly. "But how are they using this much magic to start with? This felt like it was a structured spell, and I don't know how they did it."

"A handful of witches and occultists figured this out," Zelda said looking thoughtful for a minute. "Iggatol comes to mind, it's why as a community we've chosen to not share his complete works uncensored. Pendleton dabbled as well, though he only wrote half of it down. The Duerson sisters also cracked it. Those are just the ones I know off the top of my head."

"So either we're dealing with occult experts who know how to unlock secrets..." Mia started.

"Or they've found someone's work through an obscure or rare book," Zelda nodded. "And I suspect you're not dealing with the former."

"Yeah, you're probably right," Mia agreed.

"On the upside, it's highly unlikely that a shadow would go after anyone but the idiots wielding it," Zelda said thoughtfully. "But when something like that comes into this world you can never be sure what it will do, especially once its consumed its initial prey. The more they do this kind of magic, the more emboldened it may become."

"It's pretty clear that someone needs to stop them," Mia said. "But I still need to figure out who all is involved to begin with. With this much power, it's got to be a group, and I only have one possible suspect right now... and I'm not even sure if she's the person I'm looking for."

"Maybe follow the book and not the person?" Zelda suggested. "The Duersons, Pendleton, Iggatol... most of the original copies of their writings are in collections and archives. Figure out what they got a hold of, and if you can confirm they have it, you'll know you have the right person."

"Not a bad plan," Mia replied. "Mostly I just want to stop them before they hurt anyone else... or draw something to this town we can't handle."

"It's like a group of six year olds with a nuke," Zelda said, running her hand through her white hair. "You better get it out of their hands before they accidentally set it off. Power like that is seductive and corrupts your mind slowly. They may not be able to stop on their own."

"I think I may know something about that kind of power," Mia said, looking downwards. "And exactly how bad things need to get before you realize how far gone you are."

"Zelda?" a man's voice called out from down the hall. "I hate to complain, but I'm starting to get a bit cold here."

"Oh just hold your horses, Harry," Zelda yelled back. "I'll be with you in a minute."

"What is… what is happening?" Mia blinked a few times.

"Oh you caught me while I was 'entertaining,' dear," Zelda said with a wry smile. "I'd introduce you, but Harry's a bit… tied up right now. And naked. He's very, very naked."

"Uh, so I should get going?" Mia said.

"Yes dear, probably," Zelda smiled. "Like I said when you arrived, you really should have called first."

Chapter 5

Bobbi Crawford perched at her usual haunt, a secluded table in the far corner of Garrity University's library. Her laptop cast an anemic glow over the fortress of texts that surrounded her like battlements against the outside world.

"Yeah, become a history major, Bobbi... it's a great idea," she muttered, flipping through the pages of a book with a skeptic's scrutiny. "The past will come alive for you, and not suck you dry of the will to live."

There was a quiet comfort to the buzz of the fluorescent bulbs overhead. While the old part of the library was full of picturesque rows of dark wooden shelves with beams of sun piercing through skylights, Bobbi preferred the bright artificial light and beige metal shelves of the "new wing" which had been built some time in the late seventies. She used to try and study back in her dorm room, but every time she did she'd get distracted. The garish brightness of this part of the library and its relative silence was the only place she ever managed to get work done without getting side tracked.

It also helped that hardly anyone came back to this part of the library unless they absolutely had to.

Most people didn't expect Bobbi to be the studious type when they first saw her. Between her flannel shirts and hiking boots, most folks would expect her to be more at home in the woods than hiding behind a pile of books. And those people had a point – maybe she *was* more at home in the wilderness. But academics were the only way she knew that could get her out of the small Michigan town she'd grown up in.

It was hard work, but Bobbi had more than proven she belonged in this academic world too.

Bobbi leaned back, stretching her arms, the crackling tension in her shoulders betraying hours of immobility. None of it was helped by how uncomfortable Mia's bed had been the last two nights either.

She closed her eyes for a moment, letting herself get lost in her memories of the night before. She imagined Mia's impish grin, the sly touch of her fingers as they brushed against hers in clandestine affection. A forbidden smile tugged at the corners of Bobbi's mouth, mixing with an undertone of frustration. She knew that spending time with Mia was never going to go anywhere, but it was a lot more fun than sleeping alone.

It *definitely* more fun than thinking about how she'd screwed things up with Blue.

"Concentrate, Bobbi," she chided herself, opening her eyes to once again confront the thick book in front of her. "This paper's not going to write itself."

It wasn't actually due for another month, but Bobbi liked to get ahead of these things. She knew for a fact that a lot of her classmates wouldn't start this assignment until the night before, but Bobbi couldn't work like that. She needed to take her time and get things right. It's how she'd made it as far as she had.

A shift of movement caught Bobbi's attention, and she looked up for a moment realizing she was no longer alone.

A young woman glided past her table with the grace of a dancer. She was beautiful, with long black hair and fair skin, dressed in simple yet form fitting clothing. Her presence was like a spark in dry kindling, and Bobbi was on fire. Her delicate fingers lingered on the nearby shelves, her sharp blue eyes scanning the the books looking for something. Bobbi couldn't help but linger on the curve of her hip and the way her hair cascaded down her back like a silky waterfall.

God damn.

The young woman noticed Bobbi's attention, and Bobbi quickly averted her gaze back to her laptop. Bobbi's heart pounded in her chest in the hopes that this woman wouldn't see that her face was turning as red as her hair.

"Reading anything good?" the woman's voice asked, her voice a low thrum that resonated with a playful challenge. Bobbi looked up and saw that the dark haired girl was addressing her directly.

Panic set in immediately.

"Um, depends on what you consider 'good,'" Bobbi responded, leaning back in her chair and trying to fake some confidence. "If you mean a second hand retelling of a centuries-old power struggle that changed the course of history, then yeah, jackpot."

"I mean, depending on who's telling the story, that could go either way," the woman said with a wink. "Even the most fascinating things can be made boring by a bad storyteller."

"True. Some of the guys who wrote these things down seem determined to drain any excitement from this stuff," Bobbi clicked her pen, a rhythmic counterpoint to the drumming of her pulse. "And what's your interest in my... research?"

"Curiosity," the young woman said, her blue eyes glinting with a bit of mischief. "Mostly just curious about the redhead in flannel who was staring at me. I'm Lisa. Lisa Farris."

"Bobbi. Bobbi Crawford. And you know what they say about curiosity killing the cat." Bobbi couldn't believe she said something that cheesy, but here she was. She might was well commit to it. She could curl up under the table and die *after* Lisa's inevitable hasty exit.

"But remember the second part of the phrase — that satisfaction brought it back." Lisa smiled while leaning forward. "But achieving satisfaction can take a bit more work."

"I don't think anyone's ever left unsatisfied with my work," Bobbi replied, internally cringing so hard at what she had just said. Maybe she didn't have to wait for Lisa to leave to curl up and die. Maybe she could do that right now and save some time.

On the other hand, no matter how embarrassing she was being right now, *it seemed to be working.*

"Oh, that sounds like quite the challenge." Lisa leaned in closer, the faint scent of jasmine weaving a spell in the sterile library air. "History major I'm guessing?"

"What clued you in, the massive pile of history books?" Bobbi said, brushing a lock of hair out of her eyes. "Or maybe the deep frustration and lack of sleep?"

"The former was a pretty big clue, I'll admit," Lisa's laugh was a silken caress that threatened to unravel Bobbi's composure. "How much of a mess is the history department right now? They're still trying to replace Dr. Smith, right?"

"Yeah, it's pretty rough when the head of the department disappears halfway through the fall semester," Bobbi replied. "It's kinda screwed up the whole academic year."

"Yeah, that was incredibly weird," Lisa nodded. "I wonder what happened to him?"

Bobbi, of course, knew *exactly* what happened to Dr. Carson Smith. She was Facebook friends with the woman who cut his head off, and had just spent the last two nights in bed with the witch whose plan made it happen. But telling the random hot girl you just met that the missing history department head had secretly been a vampire trying to take over the world didn't seem like the best move at this exact moment.

"Bit of a mystery there, yeah," Bobbi said, trying not to give anything away.

Like that vampires were real.

"Well they say Parrish Mills is a mysterious place, and mysterious things happen." Lisa's hand hovered near Bobbi's stack of books, electric in its proximity to touch.

"Mystery can be good," Bobbi smirked, doing her absolute best to keep her voice steady. "But I find being open and direct gets better results."

"Oh, I can be very direct when I want to be." Lisa's voice dropped to a husky whisper, her gaze locked onto Bobbi's.

"Promises, promises," Bobbi murmured, her laughter a defense against the dizzying pull of Lisa's gravity. "So what exactly are you majoring in, Ms. Lisa Farris?"

"English, with an emphasis on creative writing," Lisa said, her finger tips brushing the edge of Bobbi's. "How people's stories are told is probably my favorite thing. The way you choose to frame a story can cast the hero of one person's tale as the villain of another's."

"Perspective can color how we look at things for sure," Bobbi nodded. "But sometimes in real life there really are absolutes. Like there are lines folks can't cross."

"I don't know," Lisa shrugged. "Where those lines are vary — and just because someone's crossed those lines doesn't make them irredeemable."

"Yeah, that's true sometimes, but there *are* people who are so far gone, you can't really redeem them," Bobbi said, leaning back in her chair.

"Do you really think so?" Lisa said, cocking her head. "I think there's at least *some* hope for everyone. I don't think anyone's *truly* irredeemable."

"I disagree," Bobbi shook her head. "There are folks in this world where there's no going back from what they've done."

"Give me one example," Lisa smirked. "I just want a single example of a truly irredeemable person. I bet you can't."

"Okay, I'm just going to say it — Hitler," Bobbi replied. "I think that Hitler was truly irredeemable."

"Okay yeah, Hitler," Lisa nodded with an embarrassed grin. "God it's sad how that just eviscerated my point."

"That's the thing with real life," Bobbi said. "Sure, nuance is important like ninety percent of the time, but sometimes Hitler's just Hitler."

"I'm going to write that down," Lisa smirked. "Put it on a T-shirt or something."

"Ah yes, the burgeoning Hitler T-shirt market," Bobbi laughed. "I don't think you'll get the customers you actually want for that."

"Okay, another good point," Lisa shook her head. "God, you are just demolishing me, Bobbi Crawford."

"If only I could demolish this paper," Bobbi sighed.

"Well okay then, I get the hint. Keep studying, history buff," Lisa said, straightening up and casting one last smoldering look over her shoulder. "But don't get too lost looking backwards, because usually the best stuff is waiting for you in the future."

"Looking forward to it," Bobbi replied, her gaze clinging to the retreating form of Lisa Farris like a lifeline in tempestuous waters. *Looking forward to it? That was about the dumbest thing you could say. What does that even mean?* thought Bobbi, chastising herself.

She watched as Lisa paused to grab a book off a nearby shelf and then navigate her way through the labyrinth of the stacks. Lisa's movements were a silent symphony of confidence and grace. God Bobbi hoped she hadn't messed that up.

"God damn it, Crawford, stop," Bobbi chided herself quietly, her voice lost in the vastness of the library. "Just get your shit together and get back to work."

Chapter 6

Mia's stomach was filled with a pit of unease as she entered Riley's cluttered office at Garrity University. The soft glow of the desk lamp cast an eerie dance of shadows on the walls of the small room, doing little to make her feel better. Riley looked up from her desk, as Mia closed the door behind her.

"So I'm about to your day a whole lot worse," Mia began, the tension in her voice clear. "The magic being used by whoever or whatever group killed Greg? It's powerful enough to draw something truly dangerous." She hesitated, swallowing hard before continuing. "A true shadow."

"I have no idea what that is, but it doesn't sound good," Riley said, leaning back in her chair and rubbing her temples.

"It's not," Mia sighed, sitting in the chair across from Riley's desk. "It's the opposite of good. I'll give you the full explanation later, but the short version is 'big scary thing that consumes all life it comes into contact with.'"

"Well I look forward to the nightmares it's going to give me once you explain it," Riley said shaking her head. "The deeply scary, scary nightmares."

"When it freaks out the woman who lives in a haunted house, you know it's scary," Mia said, pulling off her winter coat. "Any luck on your end though?"

"Yeah, I think I might have found something too," Riley replied. She pulled up an old email on her computer and turned the screen to Mia. "There was a memo a few months ago I forgot about, and it might be important."

On the screen was an internal memorandum noting the theft of a book from the university library's rare books collection dated from the prior November.

"Wait, does this say that Garrity University had the hand written original copy of Aesop Iggatol's Grimoire?" Mia said, her voice tinged with shock.

"Yeah, I don't know much about your magic stuff, but I remembered that name from when you banished Mason Blackwood," Riley said, brushing a strand of her blonde hair out of her face. "It slipped by me when it happened back in the fall, but obviously this is important."

"More than you know, Riley," Mia said. "I'm just shocked the university *had* that in the first place. What are the odds even... I use a copy of the *censored* version. That book has the exact kind of magic in it that could be causing all of this."

"It apparently wasn't in the collection very long," Riley replied. "It was donated to the library just a few months earlier."

"That's odd," Mia furrowed her brow. "Out of all the places the book could end up, why is it here?"

"The University has a bunch of weird stuff if you look into it," Riley shrugged. "I think maybe that's a puzzle for another day when we aren't dealing with magical murder."

"Yeah, let's focus on the people who tried to tear a frat guy out of reality, and the danger that follows it," Mia agreed.

"This whole situation is a lot, Mia," Riley sighed. "Do we need to call in backup?"

"Like who do we call, Riley?" Mia asked dejectedly. "Like who in our rolodex could possibly help us with this?"

"I don't know? Lucy?" Riley suggested. "She has to have come across something like this with how long she's been alive."

"I don't want to get Lucy and her... 'trainees' involved," Mia said. "They're trying to lie low right now, and hanging out around crime scenes isn't something they'd risk... considering how many bodies dropped back in the fall."

"How about Sarah then?" Riley said. "She's been around the block a few times."

"And I just finally got things settled with Sarah," Mia sighed. "I don't want to rock that boat. I don't think she could help anyway."

"And you're sure this isn't just you letting your personal feelings get in the way?" Riley asked, raising an eyebrow.

"Sarah can't really use magic anymore, and she never knew a lot of the theory side," Mia explained. "If this was about kicking the crap out of someone, Sarah's the one to call. I just don't think this is something we can punch our way out of."

"Fair enough," Riley conceded. "I just want to make sure we're not leaving anything on the table just because you're too scared to deal with something."

"What? Me? Avoid my feelings? Never," smiled Mia with a tinge of sarcasm.

"Yeah, you're the paragon of healthy relationships," Riley laughed. The tension briefly broke as the two friends sat in comfortable silence.

"I really miss Sarah," Mia sighed, slumping in her chair. "She'd be absolutely useless at helping us right now, but she'd yell at me to 'focus' every five minutes to make up for it."

"When's the last time you spoke to her?" Riley asked.

"When she was here back in October?" Mia said. "We started following each other on social media — does that count?"

"It does not," Riley said definitively. "You are so hung up on her."

"I mean, we were together for over a decade, so yeah," Mia replied. "You don't put something like that behind you easily."

Silence took the room again while Mia sat in her thoughts for a moment.

"Okay, I need to confirm some more of this stuff," Mia said shaking her head and rising to her feet. "I mean, I can't think of any other explanation, but I want to be sure. I'm going back to where we found the body."

"And that will tell you what?" asked Riley, looking slightly confused.

"I saw that sigil where we found Greg's body, and I want to see if there are any others," Mia said, leaning forward on Riley's desk. "Iggatol's techniques that I'm familiar with usually require multiple focal points, so if his secret stuff is similar there needs to be more than just the one on the ground."

"Well, do what you need to do," Riley said. "Be careful though."

"Careful is my middle name," Mia replied, flashing a wry grin that didn't quite reach her dark brown eyes. In truth, she could feel the dread coiling tight in her chest – but she'd be damned if she let it show.

"Right," Riley snorted. "And I'm the King of Spain."

"Your Majesty," Mia teased with an exaggerated bow before slipping out of Riley's office and into the gathering dusk.

****

The wooded park by the Wabash River was bathed in shadow, but the evening light reflecting off of the snow covered ground still felt brighter than the moon overhead. Mia shivered as she stepped onto the frozen earth, the chill air clinging to her skin like an icy caress. She could still feel the remnants of what happened here; the air still thrummed with the unmistakable hum of lingering magic over a day later.

"Show me what you're hiding," she murmured, her breath fogging in the cold. Her senses stretched wide, probing the darkness for any trace of the perpetrator's presence.

Slowly, deliberately, Mia began to comb through the crime scene, her fingers brushing against the barren winter trees, each touch a whisper of connection between her and the world around her. She could taste the tendrils of power still woven through the air, their bitter tang leaving a metallic sting on her tongue.

For this amount of energy to still be sitting in the ambient air was terrifying. This kind of spell work could be a magnet for all sorts of horrors, not just the shadow that she feared, and Mia knew she needed to stop whoever was doing this before it was too late. One spell like this might escape notice, but if whoever did this continued, things could get very bad very fast.

She quickly located the remains of the sigil she'd found earlier on the ground. It had been stepped on several times, likely by the police, but it was still distinct enough to make out. She stood and looked around for signs of other potential focal points.

She started scouring the earth along the river bank to no avail, doing her best to keep her footing and not fall into the icy, rushing current.

"Come on," she muttered to herself, frustration mounting as her search yielded nothing new. "There has to be something here..."

And then, as if in answer to her plea, she spotted it: an almost imperceptible mark, half-hidden by the snow drifted against the base of a nearby oak. Her heart leapt into her throat as she crouched down to examine it more closely.

"This is definitely looks familiar," she muttered darkly. The complex sigil on the tree almost seemed to hum, as thought it was a high tension power line. This was definitely Iggatol's work. Whoever did this had to be the same person who stole the grimoire from the library, and Lisa Farris was looking more and more like the likely suspect. The timeline of the book's disappearance and Lisa no longer coming to the shop lined up. She must have stopped searching through the occult texts in Markov Books because she found something better.

The real questions were how on earth was Mia going to confirm and prove Lisa did it, and who all was helping her. There was no way a spell like this was done alone.

Mia kept searching for more signs. Her hands carefully brushed away the snow, revealing more intricate symbols etched into the ground. The sigils were faint, as if intentionally concealed, but Mia's trained eye picked up on the subtle traces of magic that still lingered around them. She traced her finger along the lines, feeling a faint thrum of energy beneath her touch.

All of this fit into Mia's understanding of magical theory. She could see elements that were straight from rituals she had done herself, but twisted in strange and unnatural ways. This was it.

And it meant things were going to get so much worse.

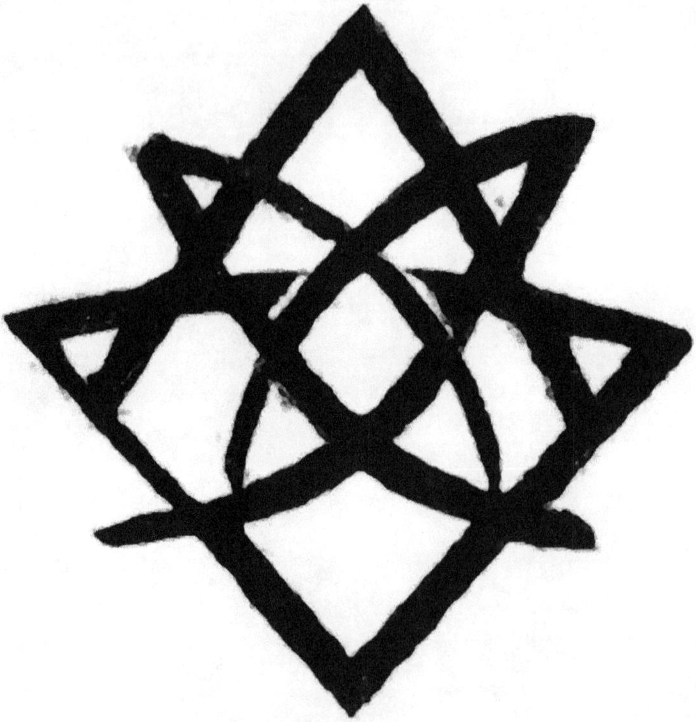

Chapter 7

"And you're sure we can't just toss a bag over her head and interrogate her in my basement?" Riley asked, pacing the creaking floorboards of Markov Books.

"Pretty confident that would get us arrested," Mia stood by the counter, her arms crossed and eyes deep with concern. "It doesn't take a law degree to know the police usually frown on kidnapping coeds."

"Bah, the cops in this town are terrible at their jobs," Riley shrugged. "We'd get away with it."

"I just don't know how we find out who she's working with," Mia sighed, leaning on the counter. "Her social media has been completely dark for months. There are zero clues online."

"You *could* just go warn her," Riley shrugged. "If she knew the dangers, maybe she'd stop? We could deal with the fact that she's a murderer *after* we make sure she doesn't draw some awful shadow thing into our world."

"I'm just afraid that would paint a target on us," Mia said, shaking her head. "This kind of magic... it clouds your judgment. Makes you think people are out to get you."

"Especially since we *are* literally out to get her," Riley replied, putting her hands on her hips. "Okay, so maybe you befriend her? You're cool and hip?"

"Except she knows I run this store," Mia responded. "She'd be suspicious immediately. If I cast a powerful spell out of a stolen grimoire and suddenly some random witch acquaintance started hanging out around me with no explanation *I'd* think something was up. Also I aged a thousand years the moment you described me as 'hip.'"

"So who do we know who wouldn't draw suspicion?" Riley said, stepping towards Mia. "Maybe someone college aged who we trust? Someone who has shown they can take care of themselves in supernatural fight? Someone with red hair?"

"I don't know if I want Bobbi to get involved with this," Mia sighed. "I don't like dragging her into this part of my world."

"You know, you've said stuff like that before," Riley replied. "But if I hadn't 'dragged' Bobbi into this stuff last fall, you'd be dead right now."

"I know," Mia looked away. "Bobbi *is* our best option. I just really wish it didn't have to be her though."

"Don't think she can handle it?" Riley asked. "Bobbi's a big girl capable of making these choices for herself."

"Yeah, but I still don't want to see her get hurt," Mia replied. "I'll text her to meet us at your house. We need to fully loop her in."

"Why my house?" Riley asked.

"My place doesn't have seating for more than two," Mia shrugged. "Also I live in a studio apartment, and I don't want to have this conversation in my bedroom."

****

Bobbi sat on the couch in Riley's living room. She'd never been to the notorious Rose House before, and it was certainly an intimidating structure. A large old victorian with an infamous past full of death and horror, the Rose House's halls were filled with the lingering souls of those who had died within its walls.

It was a little mind boggling to think that *Riley Whittaker* of all people, the most clean cut person she'd ever met, lived here.

Mia and Riley had just spent the last twenty minutes explaining that Lisa Farris of all people might be responsible for Greg Van Buren's recent death. Lisa Farris. The young woman Bobbi had just met the other day in the library. *That* Lisa Farris. It just didn't make sense, and she was still processing that when Mia suggested Bobbi infiltrate Lisa's circle of friends.

Bobbi had stopped paying attention altogether when Mia said that, and she only now realized that Mia and Riley were still talking to her.

Shit.

What were they even saying? Bobbi nodded to make it look like she understood, and hoped she'd be able to jump in soon.

"So are you comfortable with this?" Mia asked, leaning forward and letting her dark hair fall into her face a little bit. She tucked a black curl behind her ear and gave Bobbi a little smile.

This wasn't fair. Bobbi was incapable of saying no to Mia when she smiled like that.

Bobbi swallowed hard, trying to ignore the fluttering in her chest caused by Mia's smile. "Yeah, I'm comfortable with it," she managed to say, her voice shaky. "I mean, if it means preventing more deaths I'll do what needs to be done."

Riley raised an eyebrow, a hint of skepticism in her expression. "Are you sure about this, Bobbi? You know it won't be easy. Lisa might be dangerous if we're right."

"I know," Bobbi replied, determination gleaming in her emerald eyes. "But I can handle myself, and you two will have my back, right?"

Mia nodded, her smile fading slightly. "Of course, Bobbi. We'll be right there with you every step of the way."

"I've met her, you know," Bobbi said, looking up at Mia and Riley. "She seemed nice. All of this is a bit weird."

"If you don't want to do this, we can find someone else," Mia said quietly.

"No, I can do it," Bobbi said with a nod. "It's just... last time you guys roped me into this kind of thing, we were dealing with literal monsters. I can deal with monsters. I can *shoot* monsters. Lisa's a normal person."

"It's more complicated for sure," Riley said, sitting down next to Bobbi. "But all we really need you to do is spend some time with her and find out who her covenmates are and if they have Iggatol's grimoire. You don't have to do anything else."

"You know I wouldn't ask you to do this if I didn't think you could do this," Mia said, placing her hand on Bobbi's knee.

God damn it. That was just plain unfair.

"Let's do this," Bobbi said with a nod, sounding far more confident than she felt.

****

Bobbi walked through the Garrity University student union attempting to look as casual as possible. *How does someone even "look casual?" How does that even work?*

Bobbi shook her head, and tried to focus. Based on what she'd been able to glean from social media, she knew Lisa often had lunch alone in a small cluster of couches on the second floor. It was a gamble, but it was the only approach she could think of that wouldn't make her look like a crazy person.

She'd also figured that out *before* Mia had asked her to spy on Lisa.

With a deep breath, Bobbi made her way up the stairs to the second floor of the student union. As she reached the landing, she spotted Lisa sitting alone on one of the couches, scrolling through something on her phone. Bobbi approached cautiously, trying her best to exude a sense of confidence and nonchalance that were a complete and total fiction.

"Hey, mind if I join you?" Bobbi asked "*casually*," gesturing to the seat next to Lisa.

Lisa looked up, surprised by Bobbi's sudden appearance. She hesitated for a moment before giving a small smile and nodding.

"Sure, go ahead," Lisa replied, slightly cautious herself. "Bobbi, right? Wasn't sure I was going to see you again."

"Yeah," Bobbi smiled, sitting down in the sofa across from Lisa. "I don't mean to bother you, it's just cold as balls outside and I don't want to hike back to my dorm — especially since I'd have to come back for class in three hours."

Lisa laughed, "Yeah, this time of year makes me wish I'd gone to college in California or something."

Bobbi chuckled, glad that Lisa seemed to be receptive to her presence. "Tell me about it," she replied. "I'm from Northern Michigan, so I'm used to freezing my ass off, but even I have my limits sometimes."

"Honestly, some days I just want to cocoon myself in blankets and not come out until spring," Lisa smiled, her cheeks dimpling. Bobbi tried not to stare too much, but it was difficult. Lisa was beautiful even when she was buried under six layers for warmth.

So you think the troubled, dark haired witch is super hot. Bobbi chastised herself in her head. *You definitely have a type, Bobbi Crawford.*

"Yeah, I spent winter break at my cousin's cabin," Bobbi said, leaning back and trying to look nonchalant. "Three weeks just curled up by a warm wood stove, cocoa in one hand, book in the other."

"That sounds like absolute heaven," Lisa replied, tucking a lock of her long, dark hair behind her ear.

Bobbi couldn't help but get lost in Lisa's enchanting smile as she spoke. "It really was. It's rare to have that kind of peace and quiet nowadays, you know?" Bobbi said, her voice softening. "But enough about me. How about you? What did you do over the break?"

Lisa's expression shifted slightly, her smile faltering for a moment before she regained her composure. "Oh, nothing much," she replied, her tone guarded. "Just spent some time with family and friends back home. Way less cozy than what you did."

Bobbi sensed there was more to the story, a hidden sadness behind Lisa's eyes. She decided to tread carefully, not wanting to push too hard and risk scaring her off. "Family can be both a blessing and a curse sometimes," Bobbi said gently, her voice filled with empathy. "I've had my fair share of complicated relationships."

Lisa's gaze softened as she met Bobbi's eyes. "You have no idea," she murmured.

"I grew up the one openly queer kid in rural Michigan, trust me, I know," Bobbi said quietly. "Part of why I was at the cabin was that I'm actively avoiding about two thirds of my relatives, and in a town as small as the one I'm from that's pretty hard."

"That's... that's rough," Lisa sighed. "Wish I had something to say that would make that better?"

"Eh, it's okay," Bobbi smiled. "Life dealt me these cards, and thankfully the third of the family that still likes having me around includes my dad."

"Are you close with him?" Lisa asked, seeming genuinely interested.

"Yeah, he was up at the cabin with me," Bobbi nodded. "My mom passed away when I was a kid, so it's been just him and me since then. He keeps trying to get me to come home for a weekend to go ice fishing lately."

"Ice fishing?" Lisa crinkled her nose in faux disgust. "I can't imagine doing that. The cold, the *fish*."

"Oh don't knock it till you try it," Bobbi said with a wink. "Mostly you sit out on the ice getting drunk. Most kinds of fishing are just an excuse to get drunk when it comes down to it."

"Now getting drunk I can appreciate," Lisa replied. "But I feel like that's something you can do without freezing your ass off."

Bobbi laughed, her heart warming at Lisa's light-hearted response. "True, true. Ice fishing definitely isn't for everyone. But there's something oddly satisfying about the quiet solitude without a soul for miles. Just you and nature, and nothing else."

Lisa raised an eyebrow. "You make it sound almost romantic," she said, a playful smile tugging at the corners of her lips. "The outdoorsy girl with her nose buried in a book... you certainly are a puzzle, Bobbi Crawford."

"Oh, I'm pretty easily solved," laughed Bobbi.

Lisa was so easy to talk to. Bobbi was genuinely having a hard time believing this girl was the dangerous mastermind Mia and Riley thought she might be. Time would tell though.

"So, I have to get to class," Lisa said, standing up. "But I really enjoyed talking to you. Y'know, a friend of mine is having a thing over at her house tonight. Would you want to come with? It could be fun."

"Yeah," Bobbi said, looking up at Lisa. "That sounds cool."

"Great, give me your phone," Lisa smiled, seeming almost nervous. Bobbi tentatively handed it over, as Lisa punched in some information. "There, I put myself in your phone and texted myself to get your number. I'll get you the details when I'm done with class."

"Cool cool," Bobbi smiled. "I'll see you tonight."

****

Bobbi stood outside an unassuming house in the student neighborhood. The thump of bass resonated in her chest as she approached the front porch. A couple of guys sitting in lawn chairs seemed to ignore her as she opened the front door.

Inside, the living room was packed with people, the smell of cheap beer emanating from a sea of red plastic cups. Bobbi scanned the crowd looking for any sign of Lisa.

Bobbi spotted her near the back of the room, engaged in conversation with a group of people. Bobbi made her way through the crowd, feeling eyes on her as she navigated past groups of fellow college students. The music grew louder, the air grew thicker with the scent of sweat and alcohol.

As Bobbi reached Lisa's side, she realized that Lisa was immediately introducing her to the others. "This is Bobbi," Lisa said with a smile. "Bobbi, meet some of my friends. This is Mark and Theresa. Theresa lives here."

Bobbi smiled warmly and raised her hand slightly in a small, sheepish wave. "Nice to meet you both." Bobbi was not a "party" kind of person, and the whole thing was a little overwhelming.

Mark, a bespectacled young man with a nervous energy about him, returned Bobbi's wave. "Hey there," he mumbled, his voice barely audible over the pounding music.

Theresa, on the other hand, was much more animated and exuberant. With her bright pink hair and bohemian attire, she seemed to radiate energy. She immediately pulled Bobbi into an awkward hug. "Nice to meet you too!" she exclaimed, her voice filled with genuine enthusiasm.

"I'm glad you came out Bobbi," Lisa smiled. She paused and looked at Bobbi like she was considering something. "It's kind of loud in here, you guys want to move up to Theresa's room or something?"

"Sounds like a plan," Theresa smiled.

Bobbi followed Lisa, Mark, and Theresa up the creaky staircase to Theresa's room. As they entered the cramped space, the thumping bass from downstairs softened to a faint rumble. The walls were adorned with posters of bands Bobbi had never heard of, and an eclectic collection of witchcraft books lined a small bookshelf in the corner.

"Make yourselves at home," Theresa said cheerfully, plopping down on her unmade bed. "Sorry for the mess."

"No worries," Bobbi replied, taking a seat on the floor. "My room looks like a tornado hit it most of the time."

Lisa settled herself next to Bobbi, their shoulders lightly grazing against each other. "Sorry if this was too much, you were looking a little overwhelmed down there," Lisa whispered.

"Thanks," Bobbi said quietly, making brief eye contact with Lisa.

"So, Bobbi, you're a history major, right?" Mark asked, his voice tinged with curiosity.

"Yeah," Bobbi nodded.

"Absolutely insane what happened to Dr. Smith last semester," Theresa laughed. "The guy just disappeared in the middle of October. Have any theories about what happened to him?"

"There's an open police investigation I heard," Mark nodded. "Apparently his whole house was trashed."

Bobbi bit her lip hoping not to give anything away.

"Don't bug her about that stuff," Lisa threw a dirty sock from the floor at Theresa. "You're being weird."

"So, uh, looks like you're into witch stuff?" Bobbi asked, glancing at the book shelf.

"Oh yeah," Theresa smiled. "Do you dabble?"

"Not really?" Bobbi replied. "I... I used to hook up with someone who called herself a witch though. I've always been interested in it, but never really was brave enough to try anything myself."

"Oh, it's so awesome!" Theresa lit up and leaned forward. "Lisa, Mark, our friend Beeds, and I…" Theresa stopped talking after making eye contact with Lisa, who was giving her a look that could cut glass. "We've done some stuff, no big deal."

"I mean, that's cool," Bobbi shrugged, not pushing the issue. "Spooky stuff is cool."

"So, Bobbi," Mark piped up, breaking the awkward silence that had begun to settle over the room. "Have you ever experienced anything supernatural? Like... I don't know... seen a ghost or something?"

"I mean, not really?" Bobbi smiled. "Like I've heard stories, but never experienced anything myself. You guys ever hear about the Rose House?"

"The creepy big house in the Third Ward?" Theresa asked. "That place looks like a strong wind could blow it down. I've heard it's super haunted. There are a bunch of stories about some woman who disappeared there in the nineteen-twenties."

"Yeah, apparently Dr. Whittaker in the Poli Sci department lives there," Bobbi said. "Like if you dig into the history of the town, over two dozen people have died in that house."

"Seriously? That's insane," Mark exclaimed, his eyes widening with excitement.

Bobbi nodded. "Yeah, it's like a magnet for all things supernatural. Rumor has it that the spirits of the people who died there still linger, trapped in the house."

"Have you ever been inside?" Lisa asked, her tone casual but her eyes gleaming with curiosity.

"No, I've never had the guts to go in," Bobbi lied, as if she hadn't *just* been there. "But I've heard some crazy stories from people who have. One of my friends said she saw objects moving on their own and heard disembodied voices when she visited."

Theresa leaned forward, her expression eager. "Do you think we could go check it out? Like, tonight?"

Lisa raised an eyebrow, a small smirk playing on her lips. "Are you suggesting we break into the Rose House?"

"I mean... maybe?" Theresa shrugged, looking a little embarrassed.

"Bobbi literally just said Dr. Whittaker lives there," Mark laughed. "I'm in her international relations class. I am not getting arrested or expelled on the off chance I'd see a ghost."

"Yeah, breaking and entering into a professor's house is off the table," Lisa smiled. "You gotta stop being so gung ho on every impulse."

"You guys are spoil sports," Theresa fake pouted, leaning back on her bed.

"I mean, you could always break in and report back to us," Lisa joked. "Let us know how it goes for you. We'll be safely back here, *not* getting arrested."

"Maybe I will," Theresa laughed. "Maybe I'll break in and seduce a hot ghost. Just you wait."

The room erupted in laughter, and Bobbi joined them. If these people knew what Bobbi knew, they'd realize just how possible that could have been not too long ago.

The four of them slipped into easy conversation for the next several hours. Lisa began to lean a bit on Bobbi's shoulder, and Bobbi couldn't help but find herself enjoying the casual closeness. They kept talking even after the downstairs revelry seemed to fade away entirely.

After a while the pre-dawn light began to filter through the window.

"Oh shit, did we sit up all night?" Mark said, pulling himself to his feet. "Guess it's time to call it."

"Yeah," Lisa said groggily. Bobbi got up, and helped Lisa to her feet.

"See you guys later," Theresa smiled, lying back across the bed.

As Bobbi stepped out into the cold early morning winter air, Lisa grabbed her arm from behind.

"Walk a girl back to the dorms?" Lisa smiled.

"I mean, I could drive you instead?" Bobbi laughed, pointing at her black F-150 parked halfway down the block.

"You have a truck," Lisa blinked. "Like an actual vehicle on campus."

"Uh, yeah?" Bobbi said. "With heated seats and decent snow tires."

"Oh my god you had me at heated seats," Lisa said, running towards the truck.

Bobbi smiled, following behind. She unlocked the doors and climbed into the cab.

"I used to have a car, but some stuff happened," Lisa said from the passenger seat, shaking her head. "Been hiking everywhere lately, and it sucks."

"Well today I will be your chariot," Bobbi said, putting the truck into gear.

The drive back to campus wasn't that long, and Bobbi soon pulled into the student parking lot next to the dorms.

"I'm really glad you came out, Bobbi," Lisa said quietly as they stood next to the truck. "I think Mark and Theresa really like you."

"I like them too," Bobbi shrugged. "Thanks for asking me to join."

"This is where we head to our separate dorms, and I really need sleep," Lisa smiled. "But I feel like I'd regret it if I didn't do one more thing."

"One more th—" Bobbi could only get the beginning of her question out before Lisa grabbed her and kissed her.

The kiss was electrifying, sending a shockwave through Bobbi's body. Time seemed to stand still as their lips moved in sync, their breath mingling in the crisp winter air. Lisa's touch was tender yet passionate, her fingers softly grazing Bobbi's cheek before lingering on the nape of her neck.

As they finally pulled apart, both of them were breathless, their eyes locked in an intense gaze. In that moment, Bobbi felt a whirlwind of emotions swirling within her—desire, curiosity, and a boatload of guilt. She had never expected things to escalate like this with Lisa, but there was an undeniable chemistry between them.

"I-I should get going," Lisa said, her voice barely above a whisper. "We can talk later?"

Bobbi nodded, unable to form words as she watched Lisa retreat towards her dormitory. This little "mission" was way more complicated than Bobbi had ever expected.

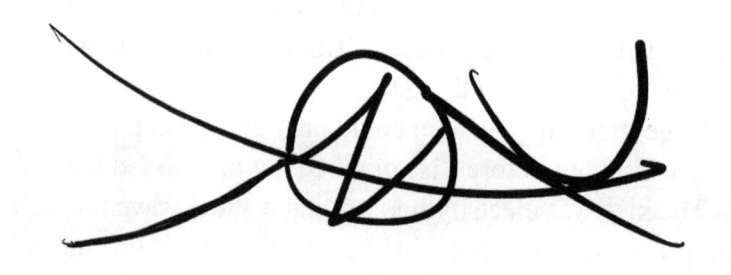

Chapter 8

"And you're sure no one saw you?" Riley asked, quietly.

"Yes, I'm sure," Bobbi said as she closed the office door behind her.

Bobbi had only been in Riley's office a couple of times, but in each visit the small, cramped room seemed to be even more increasingly covered with books and papers. Riley sat behind the desk, and Bobbi slumped herself into the one chair that wasn't absolutely buried.

"I don't like any of this," Bobbi sighed. "Is Mia absolutely certain that Lisa's the one behind Greg's death?"

"I mean, she thinks she's right," Riley nodded. "But the whole point of this is to be absolutely certain."

"It just sucks. Don't tell Mia this, but I think I kinda *like* her?" Bobbi said, looking at Riley nervously. "And I feel like I'm lying to her."

"I mean, you *are* lying to her," Riley said flatly. "We can't really get around that. Like the whole *point* is that you're lying to her. Greg Van Buren's dead, Bobbi. Please remember that."

"Yeah, it's kind of hard to forget," Bobbi replied. "They're holding a massive candlelight vigil for him tonight, now that police have publicly released the identity of the body."

"Bobbi, if we're right, these people are dangerous," Riley explained. "All we need you to do is make sure we're right about who they are."

"I know, it just sucks," Bobbi shrugged.

"So have you found anything so far?" Riley asked, leaning forward in her chair.

"Not much, I haven't talked to Lisa since I last saw her Saturday morning," Bobbi said. "I think I know who Lisa'd be working with, but not a whole lot else. I'm still working on getting her to let me in."

Bobbi purposefully neglected to mention the kiss.

"Well keep pushing," Riley sighed. "Mia's worried they might target someone else. She says people who use magic like this tend to escalate."

"Well she'd know better than the rest of us," Bobbi said, standing up. "Really wish she was doing this instead of me."

"I think we all do," Riley said, shaking her head. "Good luck, Bobbi."

"Thanks, I'll need it," Bobbi replied, leaving Riley's office. She closed the door behind her, and headed down the hall and into the busy building lobby.

"Oh, hey! Bobbi!" a voice called from behind her. Bobbi turned, and saw Lisa jogging to catch up.

"Oh, uh, hey," Bobbi replied awkwardly. *Did Lisa see where I came from? She can't have... I'm in this building all the time. The History Department is right down the hall from here. It's fine. It's gotta be fine.*

"So I just got done with class and was thinking about grabbing some lunch, want to join me?" Lisa smiled.

That smile could probably convince me to do anything, Bobbi thought to herself. "Yeah, I could eat."

"Great," Lisa said, zipping up her coat. "I end up eating alone a lot on Mondays, and it sucks."

They stepped out into the bitter cold Indiana winter, and walked to the student union. After grabbing something in the food court, the two settled in a small booth in a quiet corner.

"So I know you didn't want to talk about it the other night, but I was surprised you were into witchcraft," Bobbi said, carefully broaching the topic. "You don't really seem the type."

"I don't?" Lisa asked. "What kind of person is 'the type' in your mind?"

"Theresa," Bobbi answered. "Definitely Theresa."

"Yeah, I can see that," Lisa said with a laugh, taking a bite of her burger. "I don't know though, I've always been interested in that stuff. There's a cool store downtown if you're ever interested in that kind of thing."

"Markov Books?" Bobbi said. "Yeah, I've been in there a couple of times."

"You kinda have to dig to find the real stuff, but it's there," Lisa said. "I guess, if you're *really* interested I could maybe show you a thing or two some time?"

"I think I might like that," Bobbi nodded. She felt guilty lying to Lisa, but this was exactly the kind of thing she needed to find out right now.

"Then it's a date," Lisa smiled. "How about tonight?"

"I don't know. I was thinking about going to that candlelight vigil for that Greg Van Buren guy?" Bobbi said, trying to gauge Lisa's reaction.

"Ugh, yeah, that," Lisa said, slumping in the booth. "You know, last semester like six students died and a professor disappeared. And that's not even counting the townies? Or that freshman who got killed on Water Street in a hit and run last semester?"

"Yeah," Bobbi replied.

"Not a single candlelight vigil for any of them," Lisa continued, throwing her hands up in frustration. "But Greg? That sack of shit's dad's important, so he gets the martyr treatment."

"So, uh, you knew him?" Bobbi asked, hiding that she already knew the answer.

"Oh, you could definitely say that," Lisa said, clearly trying to calm herself. "We dated for a while, and there are things about him that most people don't know. Frankly I think he got what he deserved."

The anger in Lisa's voice was clear, and it sent a chill down Bobbi's spine.

"I'm sorry I brought it up," Bobbi said quietly.

"No, it's not your fault," Lisa said, relaxing a little. "You couldn't have known. It just sucks when everyone keeps talking about what a great person he was, when he's literally the worst person I've ever met. And, like, you can't tell grieving people that he was *actually* human garbage. Folks don't react well to that."

"I suspect they wouldn't," Bobbi said, nodding along. "That has to be hard."

"And people keep trying to be nice to me about him," Lisa said quietly. "They go 'oh, you and Greg were so close' and 'you must be hurting so much' when I'm actually secretly glad he's dead."

Bobbi sat there quietly, chewing her food. Lisa looked so vulnerable, even when she was confessing that she was happy about Greg getting murdered.

"I'm sorry that I'm unloading on you about this," Lisa muttered, slowly eating a french fry. "I just feel like I can't talk about this with my friends. Mark, Theresa, even Beeds... they just sort of look to me for guidance? Like I feel like I have to be strong for them."

"That sounds lonely," Bobbi replied.

"It kind of is," Lisa said, looking down.

"Okay," Bobbi started. "This is what we're going to do tonight. I'll come over to your place, we can order a pizza, you can show me your witchcraft stuff, and we'll pretend Greg never existed."

"I like the idea, but my roommate's got a big project she's working on," Lisa replied. "So my place is a no go."

"Then bring your stuff over to my room," Bobbi shrugged. "My roommate dropped out last semester so I have the room to myself."

"Then it really *is* a date," Lisa smiled.

****

Bobbi frantically tried to get her dorm room into some sort of presentable shape. Grabbing the dirty clothes off of the futon, she quickly shoved them into the hamper in the back of her closet.

She glanced at the clock on her wall and realized that Lisa would be arriving any minute. The nervous energy in the air was palpable as Bobbi paced back and forth, rearranging the books on her desk and tidying up a few empty bottles.

Finally, there was a knock on the door. Bobbi rushed to answer it, her heart pounding in her chest. She swung the door open to find Lisa standing there with a stuffed bag under her shoulder.

"Hey, come on in," Bobbi said, stepping aside to let Lisa enter.

Lisa smiled and walked into the room, her eyes scanning the space curiously. "Where can I put this down?"

"The spare desk's probably fine?" Bobbi pointed to am empty desk in the corner. It had been covered in trash only twenty minutes ago, but thankfully she'd managed to dispose of it before Lisa's arrival.

"Cool," Lisa said, placing the bag on the piece of cheap, fiberboard dorm furniture. "This stuff's kind of heavy." Lisa unzipped her coat, and slid it off revealing the tight, black top that clung to her slender figure. Bobbi did her best not to stare.

"So what exactly did you end up bringing over?" Bobbi asked, trying to keep focus.

"Okay, so mostly it's books," Lisa said, opening the bag. "Like if you want to get into witchcraft, you need to read some of this stuff."

Bobbi walked over to Lisa and watched the dark haired woman start pulling books out of her bag.

"So, I brought, like, some real basic stuff? Like Margot Adler's Drawing Down the Moon basic," Lisa explained. "It's a history of the modern era of the witchcraft movement. No magic, no spells – just, like, the origins of a bunch of the modern traditions. Like a lot of books from the last fifty years are soaked in nonsense, and it helps you discern if the author knows what the fuck they're talking about if you know the history yourself."

"That sounds... kind of dry?" Bobbi commented. Mia had tired to get Bobbi to read that same book the last time Bobbi asked about this stuff too.

"Oh, it is," Lisa laughed. "But, like, you gotta do the basics. And I brought the fun stuff too."

"The fun stuff?" Bobbi asked.

"Oh yeah," Lisa's smile became slightly more mischievous as she started pulling out some leather bound tomes. "So you can find like Neopagan bullshit that actually works, and I brought some of that. But if you want to do the *real* fun stuff, you gotta start digging in old grimoires and journals."

Bobbi took the leather bound book from Lisa's hands and opened its pages carefully. "What is this stuff?"

"So, like, they get real gatekeepy about this stuff online, but it's where you find some really cool stuff," Lisa explained, leaning on the desk. "So between folk magic users and weirdo occultists, people have been doing some really cool magic shit for ages. Most of this stuff is kept offline and still passed around in handwritten journals. What you're holding is a copy of a copy of a copy, transcribed in 1975 by some guy named Hamish Drucker."

"So it's *not* ancient?" Bobbi asked, flipping through the pages.

"Not this copy itself, no," Lisa said, shaking her head. "But it's a transcribed copy of Catherine Duerson's magical field theories in total. Like a lot of these things are really study notebooks from witches learning from other witches. There's a legacy to these books. Like you can feel the human connection."

"That's really cool," Bobbi said, putting the book back down on the desk. "So are we doing anything with these tonight?"

"If you want to do something tonight, you read," Lisa smirked, leaning in close to Bobbi. "You like doing homework? Well starting out is *all* homework."

"Oh, exciting," Bobbi said sarcastically.

"C'mon, you don't want to curl up with me and read old books all night?" Lisa asked, inching closer to Bobbi. "I mean, unless you want to do something else?"

Bobbi's heart was pounding as her eyes stayed locked with Lisa's.

"I wouldn't mind doing something else," Bobbi replied, her voice barely a whisper.

A mischievous smile played on Lisa's lips as she took a step closer to Bobbi, their bodies almost touching. "Well then the books can wait," she said softly.

Before Bobbi could think about what a bad idea it was, she found herself pulling Lisa into a deep and intense kiss. The passion and heat seemed to radiate from both of their bodies, and the air almost felt electric around them. The two stumbled across the room without breaking the kiss, toppling onto the cheap metal framed futon together.

Lisa's body pressed down on Bobbi's as their lips continued to move in sync. The desperate hunger between them seemed to grow stronger with each passing second, the tension building up like a storm on the horizon. Lisa started unbuttoning Bobbi's flannel shirt with trembling hands, her fingers fumbling over the buttons. Bobbi gasped as Lisa's touch grazed her bare skin, sending shivers down her spine. The room was filled with a heady mix of desire and anticipation, their bodies entwined as they explored each other with a newfound hunger.

This was probably a terrible idea. Bobbi knew this. She knew she was lying to Lisa, and that Lisa had likely done something horrific. But right now, in this moment, she found herself not caring about anything but this moment.

Bobbi felt Lisa's hands unbuttoning her jeans, and gasped as Lisa's deft fingers slid inside the waistband of her underwear, teasing and exploring. A shiver of pleasure ran through Bobbi's body as she arched into Lisa's touch.

Their bodies moved in a dance of primal need, leaving no room for apprehension or hesitation. Bobbi clung to Lisa, surrendering to the sensation. As her pleasure mounted, she could feel Lisa's breath hot on her neck, and a low, sultry voice whispering into her ear.

"I've wanted to do this since we first met in the Library," Lisa said, her voice a low growl, as her fingers continued their explorations. "I wanted to feel you, to taste you."

Bobbi moaned, her voice hoarse as her body trembled with pleasure. Just as Bobbi felt herself begin to climax, Lisa's lips found their way to Bobbi's neck, her teeth gently grazing the sensitive skin. It was a sensation that sent a jolt of electricity coursing through Bobbi's body, pushing her over the edge. Her muscles tensed and her heart pounded as she reached the peak of her pleasure.

As her orgasm subsided, Bobbi felt Lisa begin to kiss her way down Bobbi's stomach.

"Hey now, I think it might be your turn," Bobbi laughed.

"Maybe in a bit, but I'm in a giving mood tonight," Lisa laughed.

Bobbi bit her lip and closed her eyes, letting Lisa take complete control.

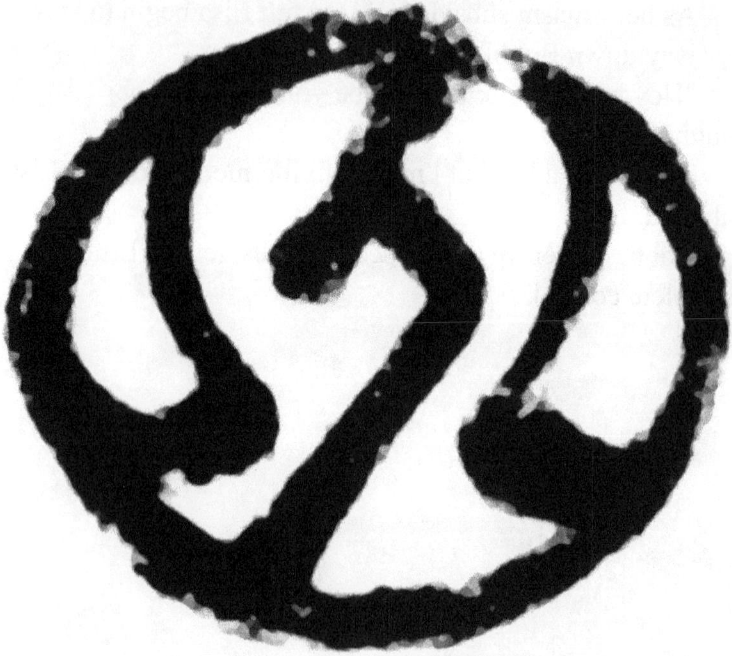

Chapter 9

Candlelight flickered in the snow as Mia and Riley arrived at the vigil for Greg Van Buren. Mia wasn't sure what they'd find here, but she had a hunch that whatever it was would be important.

Of course sometimes she had terrible instincts, so it might also be completely fruitless.

"Keep your eyes peeled, Riles," Mia murmured, her eyes scanning the sea of faces for any hint of a threat, supernatural or otherwise. Her fingers brushed against the arm of her coat, hoping she'd be able to activate her sigils through it in a pinch.

Winter was the absolute *worst*.

"Trust me, I'm on high alert," Riley replied as she studied the gathering. "No idea what we're looking for, but I'll definitely be alert when I see it."

As they wove their way through the throngs of mourners, a tall man in a well appointed suit stepped up to the makeshift podium, his figure casting an imposing silhouette against the snowy backdrop. The crowd hushed, their collective breaths held in anticipation.

"Members of the Garrity University community," he began, his voice thick with emotion. "For those of you who don't know me, I'm Thomas Van Buren. I'm... I'm Greg's father." He paused, swallowing hard before continuing.

"Greg touched so many lives during his short time on this Earth, and it's clear from the outpouring of grief and support that he made a lasting impact on this community."

Mia couldn't help but feel a pang of sympathy for the grieving father, even as her instincts screamed at her not to let her guard down. She knew all too well how vulnerable people were when they were consumed by loss.

"So far everything seems normal," Mia whispered, nodding discreetly toward Thomas Van Buren. "Just some people experiencing grief, and some other folks showing up out of social pressure."

"Or performative grief in some cases," Riley agreed, shaking her head. "But yeah, perfectly normal, non-magical stuff."

"Well we just keep watching then," Mia urged, her voice barely audible over the senator's impassioned speech. "Maybe this is just going to end up being a massive waste of time, but we can't afford to take any chances."

"Wait, over there," Riley grabbed Mia's arm. She gestured towards a young man near the front with messy blond hair and glasses. "That's Mark Durante. He's in one of my classes, and Bobbi said he's in Lisa's group."

Mark looked incredibly nervous, his body tense as if expecting danger at any moment. Mia's instincts flared, a warning bell ringing in her head. "I don't like it. He's got to be up to something."

A chill wind blew through the park, sending shivers down Mia's spine as she watched Mark's furtive movements. Her breath caught in her throat when he discreetly retrieved a small object from his pocket, barely visible in the dim candlelight.

"Riley," she whispered urgently into her phone, her voice barely audible. "Mark's got something."

"Did you see what it was?" Riley asked.

"No, but he's approaching Senator Van Buren with it," Mia replied, keeping her eyes locked on Mark.

"Shit," Riley cursed under her breath. "Don't lose sight of him. I'll try to find a way to intercept him."

Mia nodded. With a mixture of fear and determination, she continued to observe and track Mark's every move. Greg's father was deep in his passionate speech, oblivious to the possible danger that crept closer with each step Mark took.

As Mark neared Thomas Van Buren, Mia could feel the tension in the air thicken. Her heart raced, adrenaline surging through her veins as she silently willed herself to decipher the meaning behind his actions.

Damn it, what are you up to? she thought, clenching her fists. The snowflakes swirling around her seemed to mock her helplessness, their icy laughter chilling her to the bone.

It was difficult to move through the crowd, but Mia did her best to keep her eyes on Mark. As he got closer to Greg's father, Mark seemed to slip the item into Senator Van Buren's pocket.

"Riley," Mia murmured, trying to keep her voice down.

"What is it?" Riley responded, instantly picking up on Mia's distress.

"Mark Durante slipped the thing he had into Senator Van Buren's coat pocket," Mia revealed in hushed tones, struggling to keep her emotions under control. "I don't know what it is, but it can't be good."

A look of steely determination flashed across Riley's face as she nodded. But no matter how hard they tried, there wasn't really a way to make it to the front of the vigil without drawing attention.

"This sucks so much," Mia said, practically bouncing in place.

"What's your plan when we actually get up there?" Riley asked. "Oh, you might have a magic thing in your pocket, can we take a look?"

"I don't know, maybe we wait until it's over?" Mia suggested. "Intercept Van Buren before he leaves?"

"That's a when, not a what," Riley replied. "Like what's our *actual* plan?"

"Fuck if I know," Mia shook her head. "I figured I'd crack that egg when I got to it."

"You're really inspiring confidence here, Graves," Riley sighed.

"Don't I always," Mia said under her breath.

When the vigil eventually ended, the crowd began to disperse. As Thomas Van Buren headed towards the parking lot, Riley and Mia began to follow, trying to keep him in view.

Mia moved like a shark, sliding through the throng of mourners as fast as she could. With Riley not far behind her, she was quickly closing the distance. Van Buren was almost in reach, when without warning, Mia accidentally bumped into the shoulder of an unsuspecting young woman, sending her sprawling to the ground.

"Oh my god, are you all right?" Mia asked, reaching down to help the young woman up.

"I... uh... yes?" replied a meek voice. The young woman pulled a scarf down, and Alexis of all people stared back up at Mia. "I'm sorry Mia, I didn't see you there."

"It's okay Alexis," Mia sighed, pulling the young woman back up to her feet. "I'm the one who should apologize. I'm the one who bumped into you."

"It's okay," Alexis said, brushing herself off. "I've got to get going, I'll see you at work tomorrow?"

"Yeah, tomorrow," Mia nodded. As Alexis scampered off, Riley managed to catch up.

"Did you get to him?" Riley asked, breathing a little hard.

"No," Mia shook her head, as she watched Van Buren's car drive away. "Accidentally demolished one of my employees instead and missed him."

"God damn it," Riley shook her head. "Why are we so bad at this?"

****

Mia slumped in the well worn wooden chair in the back corner of the Drunken Siren. Tonight had been an abject disaster, and she really needed to drown her sorrows. Riley soon arrived at table with their drinks in hand, and settled in across from Mia and sighed.

"So we're just doing amazing, huh," Riley said, shaking her head. "If a state senator goes up in flames as he's torn from reality, I'm going to feel like shit."

"You and me both," Mia sighed, taking a drink. "I just don't know what we're supposed to do."

"Maybe stop pretending we're the magic police?" Riley shrugged. "Like, I'm a professor and you work retail. We are not cut out for this. Why is it our responsibility exactly?"

"Who else is going to do it?" Mia said quietly. "Like right now there's an open murder case, but the cops are trying to find out what mystery accelerant was used. And they're not prepared for the dangers that follow. If a true shadow shows up..."

"Yeah, I know," Riley replied. "I'm just frustrated that we live in a world where everything could burn down in an instant, but no one wants to believe it's real."

"I mean, isn't that just the thing?" Mia said, laughing to herself. "I could summon a lightning bolt live on the nightly news and most people would assume it's fake. Most of the darker parts of the world are absolutely shit at hiding. People just don't want to notice."

"So folks are just left with people like us," Riley shrugged.

"The worst part?" Mia said, pushing one of her dark curls out of her face. "These are just normal, ordinary kids who've gotten ahold of a magical nuke. They have no idea about the danger."

"Ordinary kids who *killed someone*, Mia," Riley said. "Like let's not forget that."

"I know, but I think we need to face certain realities," Mia leaned back in her chair. "When we stop them, *if* we stop them... we're not going to be able to bring them to justice. We don't have the authority to do anything, and we can't treat them like monsters."

"I know you're right, but I don't like it," Riley shook her head. "Maybe we could convince them to turn themselves in?"

"Maybe," Mia shrugged. "But the priority has to be stopping them. Things are going to get so much worse if we don't."

Chapter 10

Bobbi and Lisa laid entangled with each other on the futon in Bobbi's dorm room. Lisa curled herself under Bobbi's arm and absentmindedly traced circles on Bobbi's stomach.

What the hell am I doing? Bobbi thought to herself. This had gone too far. She was just supposed to find out whether or not Lisa had been using forbidden magic like Mia suspected. Bobbi was definitely not supposed to *sleep* with her.

This was going to end badly.

"That was nice," Lisa said quietly, nuzzling in closer. "You make me feel safe, Bobbi."

This was going to end *incredibly* badly.

"You deserve to feel safe," Bobbi replied, running her fingers through Lisa's dark hair. "I think everyone does."

"I... there's something I should tell you," Lisa said, looking up towards Bobbi's face. "About Greg."

"Okay?" Bobbi said carefully. "You don't have to if you don't want to though."

"No, I want to," Lisa sat up, her hair falling around her face. "When Greg and I were dating, we went to this party. It was fine, but I got really drunk, and since I'd driven us there I gave Greg my keys. By the time we left, I ended up passing out in the passenger seat."

Bobbi nodded slowly.

"I woke up to being slammed forward in my seatbelt," Lisa's voice was barely above a whisper. "Greg had hit... you know, the Freshman who died in that hit and run last semester? Craig Merrick?"

"Oh god," Bobbi's eyes were wide with shock.

"I was so drunk I didn't realize what happened until the next day," tears filled Lisa's eyes. "I saw the news report, and it was just... it was just too much. I went to Greg and said that he needed to turn himself in."

"I assume he refused?" Bobbi asked.

"Worse than that," Lisa was crying now, and it broke Bobbi's heart. "Greg said that if I told anyone he did it, he was going to say I was the one driving. After all, it was my car. And no one had seen us drive off."

Bobbi blinked, taking in the new information. If Lisa was telling the truth, Greg was turning out to be a very different person than most of the campus believed.

"And then, then it got worse," Lisa's voice tinged with anger. "Then his *father* called me. He told me that if I did anything that threatened his son's future, he'd see me destroyed. My car mysteriously disappeared from the parking lot that week, and I have no idea what happened to it. I think they have it."

"That's... I don't know what to say to that," Bobbi said, sitting up and wrapping her arms around Lisa. "That's so fucked up."

"That's why I'm so pissed about that farce of a vigil they held tonight," Lisa said, leaning into Bobbi. "No one cared about that kid's death, no one even remembers his name. But Greg gets their outpouring of sympathy and grief. And me? I'm just a coward."

"You're not a coward, Lisa," Bobbi said, her voice firm and steady. "You were put in an impossible situation. They took advantage of you, and it's not fair."

"I want justice for that freshman kid," Lisa whispered, her voice trembling with a determination. "I wanted Greg to pay for what he did, and I still want his father to for being complicit."

"I want to say the right thing," Bobbi said, holding onto Lisa tightly. "I have no idea what that is though."

"It's enough that you listened," Lisa whispered. "Thank you. I'm sorry for unloading like this. Can you just... can you just hold me for a while?"

"Yeah, I can do that."

****

The bright morning sun shone bright through Bobbi's dorm room window as harsh as the cold winter wind outside. Bobbi slowly awoke, blinking the sleep out of her eyes. She could feel the weight of Lisa on her side, her warm breath on Bobbi's chest.

And Bobbi's left arm was very much asleep right now.

This whole thing was a mess, and she was in far too deep. The worst part is that she really *liked* Lisa too. Bobbi felt sick, knowing that if Lisa found out that Bobbi was lying to her, it would break her heart.

She carefully extricated herself from Lisa's embrace, trying not to wake the dark haired girl. She got out of bed, hoping that the movement would bring life — and maybe some blood flow — back into her numb arm.

Bobbi grabbed one of her flannel shirts off the floor and pulled it on for warmth. Lisa's bag lay open on the desk, and it would be so easy to poke through it. She hadn't gotten a good look last night before the evening got derailed.

Bobbi glanced back and watched Lisa sleep for a moment, her chest slowly rising and falling. Turning back to the desk, she slowly opened Lisa's bag, trying not to make a sound. It really was largely just filled with books, and Bobbi started paging through a few.

She paused when she reached an old, leather bound journal. This wasn't like most of the books. It was hand written, and the pages contained intricate symbols and patterns.

"Bobbi?"

Bobbi nearly jumped out of her skin at sound of Lisa's groggy voice. She turned and saw Lisa sitting up on the futon, slowly waking up.

"Hey," Bobbi said sheepishly. "I've only been up for a minute."

"What are you doing?" Lisa asked, brushing the hair out of her face.

"Going through your stuff?" Bobbi confessed, holding up the book in her hand.

"That's certainly honest," Lisa laughed, swinging her legs over the side of the futon and standing up. She walked across the room and kissed Bobbi on the cheek. "Be careful with that one, it's over a hundred years old."

"It looks like it," Bobbi said. "How'd you get ahold of it?"

"Might have... *borrowed* it from the rare books collection in the library," Lisa smirked, pulling at Bobbi's flannel. "It's probably the most powerful grimoire out there. The transcribed versions you normally find censor like half of it."

Bobbi glanced at the signature on the inside cover.

Aesop Iggatol.

Bobbi tried not to react. She was holding the grimoire whose spells were used to kill Greg Van Buren. If there was any doubt left that Lisa was responsible for his death, it was now fully crushed. Bobbi put the book down on the desk slowly.

Lisa slid her hand under Bobbi's open shirt, and pulled her close. "Last night was nice."

Bobbi nodded nervously. "It was, yeah."

"I've got to go, I have class in like two hours," Lisa smiled. "But I'll see you at lunch maybe?"

"I have some errands to run, so I might not be on campus this afternoon," Bobbi half lied. Well, maybe not a lie at all — running over to tell Mia about what she found could *technically* be classed as an errand. "Maybe I can see you tonight?"

"Well I have a thing, so maybe tomorrow?" Lisa smiled. "We'll figure it out. Just a heads up, I don't do casual. So if you're going to break my heart, do it now."

"That's the last thing I want to do," Bobbi smiled. God, she really meant it too. She liked Lisa. She couldn't deny that she was falling for her.

She was falling for a murderer.

Fuck.

"Okay, I'm going to get going," Lisa said, collecting her clothes from the floor and getting dressed. "I'll leave a few of the beginner books here if you're curious, but that big one... that goes with me."

Lisa put Iggatol's grimoire in her bag and slung it over her shoulder. She grabbed Bobbi and pulled her into a deep kiss.

Bobbi sank into it, her heart torn in two.

She had known all of this would end badly, but this was worse than she thought.

"I'll see you later, Bobbi Crawford," Lisa said with a wink as she turned and bounced out the door.

Fuck. Fuck fuck fuck.

As soon as the door clicked closed, Bobbi started to get dressed. She grabbed her phone and dialed Mia's number, but it went straight to voice mail. Mia had probably forgotten to charge her ancient flip phone again. Riley would be teaching a class right now, so contacting her would be useless.

It was ten o'clock in the morning. Mia would be at the bookstore right now. Bobbi would just have to go tell her in person.

With her boots and jacket on, Bobbi was out the door in a flash. She'd normally walk since the store was less than two miles from campus, but she was in a hurry. Darting to her truck in the student parking lot, she drove downtown as quickly as traffic would allow.

Parking on the street, Bobbi was through the doors to Markov Books in an instant. She practically bowled over a mousy young woman who was stacking books in a rack next to the entrance.

"I'm sorry," Bobbi said hastily. "Is Mia here?"

"Yes... she's in her office?" the young woman replied. The poor girl looked like a deer in headlights.

"Sorry about that... Alexis?" Bobbi apologized, glancing at the young woman's name tag. She ran to the back and burst into Mia's modest workspace.

"Lisa has the grimoire," Bobbi said, still a bit winded. "She did it, she killed Greg."

Chapter 11

Something slithered between the walls of reality and into the cold winter morning sun of Parrish Mills. It was pure darkness, a blackness imperceptible to human eyes. It was not just the absence of light, but the absence of life itself.

It was a true shadow.

The shadow moved with purpose through the town, drawn to the flickering threads of raw, forbidden magic that some poor mortals had woven, fresh for the slaughter. It crept along the edges of buildings, slipping through cracks and crevices as if the very fabric of reality yielded to its presence.

It moved blindly, in the spaces between. It could not see its prey, but it could sense them pulsing like candles in the night.

It would take time to find them, to sink its teeth in and corrupt and consume its prey. It would take from them everything that made them whole. And then, when it was done, it could return to the void, without being burdened by this cursed existence any longer.

It would have its satisfaction, and nothing would get in its way.

****

Alexis moved closer to the back of Markov Books, trying to listen in to the heated conversation between the redheaded young woman who'd barged in and Mia. She knew Mia was looking into Lisa, and she needed to know exactly what they were talking about.

"Are you sure, Bobbi?" Mia's voice carried through the door. "You're absolutely, one hundred percent certain?"

"Positive," the other woman replied, her confident tone lacking any semblance of doubt. "I held Iggatol's grimoire in my own hands."

Bobbi. That was the name of the girl Lisa kept talking about lately. It was almost nonstop. All Lisa spoke about these days was this girl, and Alexis had been happy about it. She was happy that Lisa finally found something in her life that wasn't revenge.

But had it all been a ruse? Was Bobbi just an infiltrator sent by Mia to spy on Lisa? Had they really stooped this low?

Alexis's heart pounded in her chest, her hands trembling. This was a gross, disgusting act. Lisa needed to know how deeply she'd been betrayed. Alexis had to tell her.

She had to tell her *right now*.

As Mia and Bobbi's voices continued to echo in the back of the store, Alexis quietly grabbed her coat off the hook in the store room, and headed towards the door. With a surreptitious glance at the back, she slipped out of Markov Books, the bell above the door jingling softly in her wake.

Outside, the sharp winter sun did little to warm the chill that had settled on her soul. The icy wind whipped at her face as she hurried down the street, her breath coming in short, shallow gasps.

Lisa would be getting ready for class right now. It would take Alexis about a half an hour to get back to campus, and by then Lisa would probably be at the Union grabbing food if she went through her regular habits. She could probably text Lisa, but Alexis felt like this was the sort of thing that needed to be heard in person.

It was definitely the sort of thing Alexis would want to hear in person if it had happened to her.

As she finally stepped onto campus, she made a beeline for the union. Her footsteps echoed through the halls of the building as she entered its doors, her eyes scanning the space for any sign of her friend. Making her way to Lisa's usual corner, Alexis spotted the dark haired young woman seated alone at a table near the back, a cup of steaming coffee before her.

"Lisa," Alexis whispered, her voice barely audible above the hum of conversation around them. "I-I need to talk to you."

"What's wrong, Beeds?" Lisa asked, her expression shifting from curiosity to concern as she took in Alexis's frantic demeanor. "Aren't you usually working right now?"

"Bobbi... sh-she told Mia that she knows you killed Greg," Alexis stammered, her words tumbling over one another like a flood.

"Wait, slow down, Bobbi as in *my* Bobbi? Bobbi and Mia know each other?" Lisa said, her eyes wide with shock. "How do they know each other?"

"I don't know," Alexis admitted, wringing her hands nervously. "But she just rushed into the shop a little after ten and told Mia you had Aesop Iggatol's grimoire."

For a moment, Lisa just stared at her, her expression a mixture of confusion and fear. Then, slowly, like clockwork, Lisa seemed to put something together.

"I left her place a little before ten. I can't believe she..." she said, Lisa's voice cracking with heartbreak. "She slept with me, and then immediately ran off to tell Mia Graves. I don't understand. Was she just using me? Was I nothing to her?"

A flicker of anger danced across Lisa's face, and her sorrow slowly started to transform to rage.

"Get Mark and Theresa. Your boss knows what we're doing, so we'll need to move up the timetable." Lisa's voice held an edge of darkness that sent shivers down Alexis's spine.

"What... what do we do about Bobbi?" Alexis asked nervously.

"I don't know, I need to figure that out," Lisa said, her face a gut wrenching combination of rage and sorrow. "But we have bigger fish to fry, and I'm not letting that *user* slow me down."

"Okay," Alexis replied, averting her gaze from Lisa's piercing stare. Lisa didn't show anger often, but when she did it could get scary.

Alexis had a hard time blaming Lisa for it this time though.

****

The chill of winter crept through under the door of Markov Books. The old wooden floorboards creaked and groaned beneath Mia's feet as she paced restlessly. She stepped out from the back rooms, and looked between the shelves filled with books, crystals, and other knickknacks.

"Alexis?" Mia called out, but was met with nothing but silence. "Where the hell is Alexis?"

She should be here. She had *been* here. Where had she run off to.

Bobbi stepped out of the back. "I don't know," she said. "She was here when I first came in like forty-five minutes ago? I almost knocked her over on my way in."

Mia shook her head, the black curls of her hair dancing around her shoulders. Something didn't feel right. It was as if an icy hand had reached into her chest, squeezing her heart with an unrelenting grip.

"Do you think she overheard us?" asked Bobbi.

"I mean, probably? We weren't exactly being quiet," Mia said. "I don't know why she would have run off though."

"How well do you actually know her?" Bobbi leaned against the counter. "Like, how much does she know about your stuff?"

"I mean, I don't know?" Mia said thoughtfully. "Honestly I forget she's here half the time. She probably overheard me and Riley a few times when we discussed this stuff before."

Bobbi shifted uncomfortably. A small chime came from her pocket, and she pulled her phone out. "Oh fuck."

"Bobbi?" Mia cocked her head.

"I just got a..." Bobbi started, staring at her phone in disbelief. "I got a text from Lisa. It's... fuck. She wrote 'Beeds told me you're working for Mia. You'll pay for using me like this.'"

"Who's Beeds?" Mia asked.

"A friend of Lisa's? I haven't met her yet," Bobbi shrugged.

"Oh god damn it," Mia muttered, the wheels clicking in her head. Suddenly Alexis's disappearance made too much sense. "Beeds must be short for Biedermann. *Alexis* Biedermann. We've had one of Lisa's people working at the store this whole time."

"So she knew you were looking into her?" Bobbi looked astonished. "And now she thinks… oh god. I slept with her last night. She must think I…"

Bobbi looked absolutely sick.

"I don't think you're safe, Bobbi," Mia said quickly.

"You think?" Bobbi responded. "I just broke the heart of someone who literally used magic for vengeance against her ex. I am royally *fucked*."

"You shouldn't sleep at your place for the time being," Mia said, barely slowly down. "My place is probably a bad idea, so maybe you can stay with Riley at the Rose House or something."

"Lisa knows Riley lives in the Rose House," Bobbi said, shaking her head. "And I'm betting Alexis already told Lisa that you and Riley are friends."

"You're right, but I don't know what else to do," Mia sighed. "We shouldn't have gotten you involved in this."

"I shouldn't have slept with her," Bobbi replied. "She wasn't coming after you or Riley even though she knew you were on to her. But I fucked everything up."

"I mean, it was a dumb thing to do, sure," Mia shook her head. "But you can't exactly *un-sleep* with her. We are where we are, and we just need to move forward."

"You've got wards all over your place, it's gotta be the better option?" Bobbi suggested.

"Maybe, but it's tight quarters with one door," Mia said, glancing out the front door of the shop. "And those are designed to hide the place from supernatural beings. Lisa's a person. They might stop some of the magic, but they won't stop a determined young woman with a grudge and the ability to peel apart reality. Riley's place has multiple exits, a few warded rooms, and a bunch of ghosts who don't like to be messed with. It's our best option."

Mia went under the counter and began to rifle through a small drawer. Grabbing a handful of items, she handed a small pendant to Bobbi.

"Put this on and don't take it off," Mia said quietly. "It won't stop everything she can do, but it's a lot better than nothing."

"How screwed am I right now?" Bobbi asked, putting the pendant on. "Tell honestly, Mia."

"Oh *incredibly* screwed," Mia sighed. "We all are."

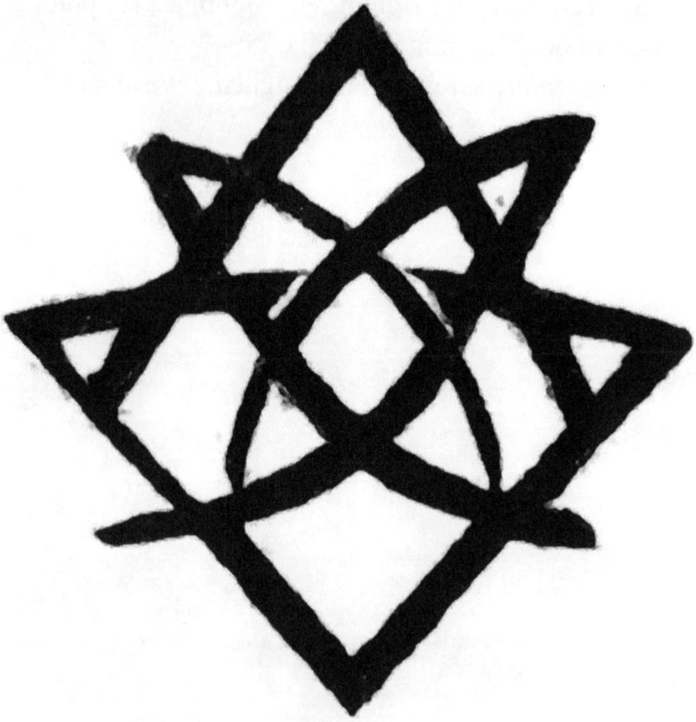

Chapter 12

Lisa sat back on the bed in Theresa's bedroom as the flickering light of scattered candles cast eerie shadows on the wall. Theresa, Mark and Alexis huddled nearby, the air thick with tension and uncertainty.

"Bobbi betrayed me," Lisa spat, her voice trembling with emotion as she fought to maintain her composure. Her face was etched with hurt and anger, her blue eyes flaring like stormy seas. She clenched her fists tightly, her dark nails digging into her palms. "Beeds probably told you, but Bobbi was working with Mia the whole time. She was just using me."

"Are you sure?" Mark asked hesitantly, his voice wavering. "How do you know?"

"I saw her talking to Mia about Lisa," Alexis said, in a voice barely above a whisper. "It... it was pretty clear."

"God, Lisa, are you okay?" Theresa asked, putting her hand on Lisa's shoulder. "Do you need anything?"

"I just need to... I don't know," Lisa said, her voice boiling over with frustration and hurt. "I just need to figure out what we do next."

"Maybe we focus on our plan then," Theresa said, trying to sound as reassuring as possible. "Bobbi never learned what we were actually doing, so there's no reason to stop."

"We've got everything we need to move forward on Greg's dad," Mark nodded. "State Senator Thomas Van Buren will never see it coming."

"The full moon is in a week," Alexis said, brushing a strand of mousy brown hair out of her face as she sat on the floor. In her lap was a notebook filled with notes and diagrams. "It's the most advantageous time for the spell. I don't think we need to move up our time table."

"I don't think we need to move it either," Lisa nodded. "So we still plan for then... but if we *did* need to change the schedule when is the soonest we could do the spell?"

"I mean, we'll be close enough in a day or two?" Alexis said, scouring a set of lunar charts. "I wouldn't want to do it any earlier. It might fail if we try it sooner."

"What if Bobbi or that Mia woman try to interfere?" Theresa asked. "What do we do then?"

"I know Mia, she's not a bad person," Alexis said quietly, her voice more timid than usual. "I don't want to hurt her."

"A good person doesn't play with people like that," Lisa snapped. "But, you're right, she's not a monster the way Greg or his dad are."

"She deserves to be slapped in the face for sure though," Theresa said. "We need a solution."

"Maybe we try to reason with her?" Mark suggested. "Tell Bobbi and Mia to keep clear of us?"

Lisa sat for a moment, her stomach forming an intense knot. Even the suggestion of seeing Bobbi right now tore her up inside like razor blades. She knotted her hands into fists again to try and keep herself under control, her nails digging into her palms so deep they threatened to draw blood.

"Okay," Lisa breathed, her voice barely audible. "We confront them, and tell them to stay out of our way."

"I think I need a beer, " Theresa said, hopping off the bed. "Anyone else want a beer?"

"I'm good," Mark said shaking his head.

"God yes," Lisa said, slumping back again.

"I know you don't drink, but do you want anything Alexis?" Theresa asked, pausing by the door. "A water? A Coke?"

"No, I'm okay," Alexis replied with a weak smile.

"I'll be right back," Theresa said, disappearing into the hall.

Something moved through the cracks in the walls, a darkness cold and malevolent, moving through the edges of reality itself.

Mark shivered, feeling the sudden sensation of ice running through his veins. It was like a cold hand had wrapped itself around his spine, leaving him rigid with fear. He glanced around the room, his eyes searching the shadows that danced at the corners of his vision, but saw nothing out of the ordinary.

"Are you alright, Mark?" Alexis asked, her voice laced with concern as she studied his pale face.

"Y-yeah," he stammered, trying to shake off the unsettling feeling that had seized him. "Just a little cold, I guess."

Theresa bounded back into the room, handing a beer to Lisa and sitting back on the bed. "Okay, so who are we sending to talk to Miss Witchier-than-thou? One of us? All of us?"

"I would rather not," Alexis said, looking at the ground. "I know that she's not our friend, but I did just walk out of work without saying anything — that felt wrong."

"*That* felt wrong? With everything we've been doing?" Theresa laughed, drinking her beer. "Man, you got some weird hangups, Beeds."

"Give her a break, Theresa," Lisa said. "Everything's a sliding scale these days. I'll talk to that Mia asshole. I'm the one who got us into this."

"I don't want you going alone," Mark said, standing up. He seemed a little unsteady on his feet, but determined nonetheless. "I'm coming with you."

"Jesus, we're not going *right now*, Mark," Lisa said, twisting the cap off her bottle of beer with the bottom edge of her shirt. "It's the middle of the night. We're not going to show up at her home."

"I don't think we even know where she lives, do we?" Theresa asked.

"Over on the corner of Blanchard Street and Winter Court," Alexis said, shrugging. "In that shitty apartment building that just makes me feel sad when I look at it."

"Why do you know that?" Mark asked, sitting back down. "I don't think I even knew there was an apartment building there."

"She made me run and get her phone charger once," Alexis shrugged. "Well, I mean she didn't *make* me, she *asked* me… but yeah. Tiny studio apartment on the first floor."

"If we go after her there, she'll think we're there for a fight," Lisa sighed, sipping her beer. "She may be an arrogant asshole, but she's powerful. I don't want her to feel cornered and, like, light us on fire."

"But we have Iggatol's grimoire, we could beat her," Mark said. Something dark flashed behind his eyes that made Lisa feel a little unsettled.

"Never assume you're the biggest bad in town," Lisa sighed. "We have power, but she's got experience. Someone like her could do more damage with a butter knife than we could with a machete."

"Her tattoos are all sigils," Alexis said, shifting uncomfortably. "She could get multiple spells off before we could even utter the first words of a ritual. We'd have to prep for hours if we thought we were going to get into showdown with her... and it'd probably take all of us to win."

"So, like, the bookstore maybe?" Theresa asked, brushing a lock of pink hair out of her face. "She'll feel like she's on home turf, but in a place where she deals with the public? It'd give you and Mark an easy exit too?"

Lisa considered Theresa's suggestion, taking a long sip of her beer before nodding slowly. "Yeah, the bookstore might be our best option. If we catch her off guard there, it's still neutral ground where we won't seem as aggressive."

Mark's gaze hardened, his knuckles turning white as he clenched his fists. "We can't let her keep poking around in our business. She needs to know we mean business too."

"You need to calm the fuck down, Mark," Lisa said, furrowing her brow. "I am pissed and I want to punch her in the face, but we need to be controlled. You can't bring that energy."

"So, tomorrow you two will go," Alexis nodded. "What do we do until then?"

"Well, tonight I want to get drunk and cry," Lisa said, downing her beer. "Maybe watch Notting Hill."

"I'll go get my laptop," Theresa sighed.

****

Lisa tugged at her scarf as she and Mark approached Markov Books. The winter air wrapping around her felt as cold as the emotional ice that was wrapping around her heart. Mark looked determined, but something was off.

There was something behind his eyes since last night that made Lisa nervous, but she brushed it aside.

They were here for a reason, and she needed to stay focused.

As they walked into the shop, the smell of incense and lavender almost hit her like a brick wall. The dimly lit store seemed more ominous than the last time she'd been here, its dark corners seeming to stretch out further than they should.

"I'll be with you in a minute," a voice called out from the back. It was her. Lisa took a deep breath and readied herself.

Mia Graves, the manager of Markov Books, stepped out of the back. She was a good half a foot taller than Lisa, and moved with dangerous grace. Even in this cold she wore a tank top, displaying the full array of spells tattooed across her body. It was clearly a display of power meant to put anyone who might challenge her in their place. As soon as Mia saw Lisa, she locked eyes and stopped in her tracks.

Lisa tried to steady herself, shaken by a mix of nerves and anger.

"We need to talk," Lisa said calmly. She was going to stay in control of this conversation if it was the last thing she did.

"I agree, Ms. Farris." Mia seemed to be looking her up and down, judging her. Her eyes shifted to Mark. "But not about what you think."

"No," Lisa said, clenching her fist. "I'm going to talk, and you're going to listen. What I'm doing is important, and you need to stay out of my way."

"You killed someone, Lisa," Mia said. "And the way you did it… I don't think you understand…"

"I don't think *you* understand," Lisa bit back. "You manipulated me. You sent Bobbi in to seduce me. That's so fucked up."

"I didn't—"

"You didn't send her in?" Lisa cut off Mia before she could finish her sentence.

"No, I did, but it wasn't—"

"So you admit it," Lisa snarled. "Good. Let's not lie about things. I'm going to finish what I started, and you're going to stay out of my way."

"I need you to listen to me," Mia said. She kept glancing at Mark nervously. Why was she looking at Mark? "You need to stop using that grimoire. The spells in there have been suppressed for a reason. There are consequences to what you're—"

"God, what is it with you people," Lisa said, rolling her eyes. "The powerful and the privileged always deciding who can do what. This kind of gatekeeper toxic bullshit is *over*."

"No, that's not what I mean," Mia said, shaking her head. "There are things I have to tell you. You're in danger."

"Are you threatening her?" Mark said in a cold, dark voice.

"No, I'm not," Mia shook her head. "The spells in that book, they can attract something called a true shadow. I think it may have already touched at least one of you."

"What are you talking about?" Lisa asked, bewildered.

"The reason that book is censored is because Iggatol broke taboos that were there for a reason," Mia said, not taking her eyes off of Mark. "There are things that kind of magic draws into this world. And once they're here, they won't stop until they hunt you down. I only know one way to stop them."

Lisa paused, considering what Mia was saying. Was it possible that she really was just worried about their well being? It seemed unlikely, but she couldn't rule out the possibility.

"How would you stop them?" Lisa asked carefully.

"If it's already in our world, and I suspect it is," Mia said to Lisa. "You need to stop using the spells in that grimoire immediately. We might be able to cast a spell on you to cloak you from it."

Lisa considered what this woman was saying. She didn't trust Mia, but she at least seemed sincere.

"But if it's already touched you... already got its hooks in," Mia paused, and looked back to Mark. "We would need to cut you off from all magic. It's the only way to stop it from destroying you."

The wheels clicked Lisa's head as she processed what Mia was saying. Suddenly so many things made sense.

"Oh my god, you're jealous of us," Lisa said quietly. "You want to strip us of our power because you're afraid we might be better than you."

"What?" Mia blinked. Of course she was stunned, it was clear Mia never would have guessed that Lisa could see through her plan.

"You just want to silence us and take the grimoire for yourself," Lisa felt tension rising through her. "Wow you're transparent."

"That is not what's happening," Mia said, stepping towards them. "I don't think your friend has much time left, Lisa. This needs to happen quickly."

"You're not going anywhere near me," Mark said, backing towards the door. "Let's go, Lisa."

"Stay out of our way, or you'll get hurt," Lisa said, almost spitting on the ground. The two were out the door in a moment, leaving Mia standing there were her mouth open.

As Lisa and Mark stepped out on the the street, Lisa began to move with determined purpose.

"That woman needs to pay for what she did to you," Mark said, keeping pace.

"Maybe, but that can wait," Lisa said quietly.

"I don't know," Mark smiled. "Sometimes lessons come sooner than expected."

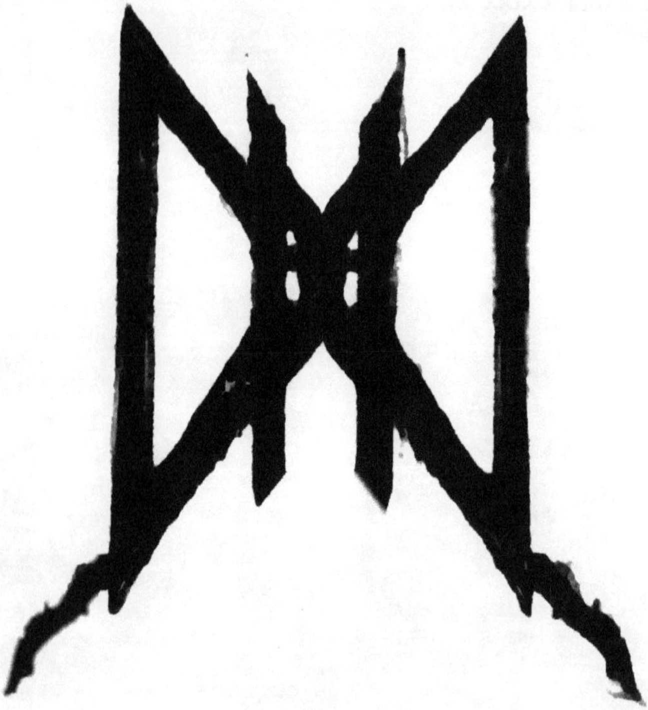

Chapter 13

Mia walked up the stairs onto the porch of the Rose House. The large Queen Anne home had definitely seen better days, its blue paint chipped and cracked. Riley had made improvements to the place since she'd moved in over a year ago, but the house had a long way to go before it would take on its former glory. With its apparent level of disrepair, most people would have second thoughts before setting foot inside.

That and all the ghosts that filled its halls probably didn't help.

Mia raised her hand to knock on the door, but it opened on its own with a creak before her knuckle could connect with the wood. The empty foyer sent a small wisp of cold that somehow chilled her more than the early winter evening.

"You know it's creepy when you do that," Mia sighed, stepping foot in to the door. "I mean, thanks for getting the door — but it's still super, super creepy."

"That you, Mia?" Riley's voice called out from somewhere deeper in the house. "I told Ben to let you in when you got here."

"Yeah!" Mia said, heading further into the house. "You get that it's weird that you ask ghosts to do stuff for you, right?"

"I don't know," Riley replied, emerging from the kitchen and wiping off her hands with a small towel. "It's their house too, and I'm just sort of used to them at this point. Also Ben likes to be helpful."

"Is Bobbi here?" Mia asked, unbuttoning her coat. "The three of us need to talk."

"She's in the study," Riley said, gesturing to a door down the hall. "She figured out that it's one of the few rooms the ghosts won't go into, so she's been hiding there."

"Riley, the ghosts one hundred percent go in there," Mia blinked. "The only rooms I warded for you were your bedroom and the upstairs bathroom."

"Yeah, but Bobbi doesn't know that and the ghosts agreed to play along," Riley smiled. "You have news?"

"Yeah, you could say that," Mia nodded, making a bee line for the study door. "Lisa Farris paid me a visit today."

Bobbi sat in a large, beaten up chair in the corner of the Rose House's study. It was the first room Riley had restored, and was wrapped in ornate wooden molding with floor to ceiling book shelves lining one of the walls. Bobbi was furiously typing on her laptop, but paused when she saw Mia enter the room.

"Okay, so things are worse than I thought," Mia said, running her hand through her dark, curly hair. "I think there's already a true shadow here, and I think it's attached itself to Lisa's friend Mark."

"That's not good," Bobbi said, putting her computer aside and standing up. "Are you sure?"

"Pretty damned sure," Mia said tossing her hands in the air. "The sigil on the back of my neck was screaming the whole time he was in the store this morning."

"This morning?" Bobbi said, astounded. "Why didn't you call or text? Why'd you wait so long to tell us."

"Your phone was dead and you didn't have a charger again, huh," Riley said, leaning on the door frame. "I told you that you just need to start keeping a spare charger at the store."

"Yes, I'm an idiot," Mia said, shaking her head. "And I couldn't leave the store since Alexis quit and I'm short staffed. Let's move past my being dumb, okay?"

"You said the shadow was attached to Mark," Bobbi said, bringing the conversation back on track. "What's going to happen to him? How long does he have?"

"Honestly? I'm not sure, the lore is vague and my only past experience with this stuff was kind of atypical," Mia said, glancing between Bobbi and Riley. "I know it's going to consume him and eventually kill him, but I don't know how long it will take. I've only seen someone get killed by one once, and no one else's done anything this dumb in like a hundred years."

"So we need to find a way to remove it from him," Riley said quietly. "How do we do that?"

"I'm not sure," Mia replied. "Everything I researched so far has been preventative. I was finding ways to hide someone from the true shadow and avoid its attention, not how to extract it from someone. Severing them from magic might work, but I'd need their consent for that to be easily doable."

"So what do we do—" Bobbi was interrupted by the sound of breaking glass from the front of the house.

"The ghosts maybe?" Mia asked hopefully, looking at Riley.

Riley glanced down the hall. "I don't think so... Hey guys? What was that?"

A gust of wind blasted down the hall, sending Riley's blonde hair into a tangled mess. Mia could hear faint whispers bound into the now cold air.

"They say someone's out front," Riley said quietly. "It's a man... they're scared of him."

"Riley, keep Bobbi safe," Mia said, her voice steeled and determined. "It's Mark. It's got to be Mark."

"Mia..." Bobbi looked concerned.

"I'll be safe, don't worry," Mia said, unsure if she believed it herself. She left the study and walked towards the front door. Pausing in the foyer, she noted the broken glass on the floor. One of the smaller window panes next to the door had been smashed with a rock, and she could see Mark's silhouette on the porch through the hole.

"Mark, what are you doing," Mia said through the broken window.

"You're all so smug, you think you know better than us," he hissed back, his voice like gravel. "It's time you and Bobbi were taught a lesson."

"Mark, you need help," Mia said slowly. "There's something attached to you, something dangerous. If we don't deal with it, you *will* die."

Mark's eyes gleamed with a manic light as he stepped closer to the broken window, his movements jerky and unnatural. Mia could feel the oppressive presence of the shadow emanating from him, the sigil on the back of her neck practically screamed.

"You think you can save me?" Mark's voice was filled with bitter mockery. "I'm not the one who needs saving."

With a flick of his hand, tendrils of darkness erupted from Mark's fingertips, snaking across the floor towards Mia like living things hungry for flesh. She quickly activated a sigil on her leg through her jeans, hoping her protective spells worked as well when she couldn't directly reach them.

When the darkness reached Mia, it hit an invisible wall, sizzling and retracting as if they were in pain.

Thank the gods that worked...

"Mark, this isn't you," Mia said, trying to stay calm. "You need to stop before it's too late."

"You don't get to tell me who I am!" Mark snapped. Darkness erupted from him, and pushed against Mia's shields. She needed to find some way to bind him, some way to contain this. The more he drew from the shadow, the less time they had to save his life.

She darted to the door, throwing it open and stood just a few feet away from Mark on the porch of the Rose House.

The night seemed to hold its breath, the air electric with tension as Mia faced Mark on the porch. Shadows swirled around him like a malevolent cloak, whispering dark promises in his ears. The true shadow's influence was palpable, twisting Mark's features into a grotesque mask of hatred and pain.

"Mark, listen to me," Mia's voice cut through the eerie stillness, laced with urgency. "The power you're drawing on right now will kill you the more you use it. You need to stop."

Mark's eyes flashed with a feral glint as he advanced towards Mia, the darkness coiling around him like a protective barrier. The true shadow reveled in his defiance, feeding off his anger and fear, urging him to unleash its full power.

In a swift motion, Mark raised his hands, sending tendrils of darkness lashing out towards Mia. The force of their collision against her defensive spells knocked her back a few feet.

Mia tossed off her jacket, the cold ripping at her as she activated a sigil on her left arm. Light exploded around her, knocking Mark onto his back.

"Mark, stay down," Mia said, readying another volley in case she needed it.

Mark scrambled to his feet, his eyes wild with a mixture of fear and determination. The true shadow's influence over him was evident in the way he moved, unnaturally swift and agile. Mia knew they were running out of time before the darkness consumed him completely.

"I don't want to hurt you, Mark," Mia said.

"I *do* want to hurt *you* though," Mark bit back.

"Yeah, no — I got that," Mia said. "You've made that incredibly clear."

Mark sent another volley of shadowy tendrils at Mia, and she managed to keep them at bay. She could feel her protections waning though. Mia honestly wasn't sure how much longer her personal shields would hold. The shadows consuming Mark were more powerful than anything she'd encountered before.

All of this seemed to be offense though. Mark was pointing all of this power *outward*, and not saving any of it to protect himself. The only reason he hadn't gotten hurt was because Mia wasn't trying to harm him.

A very simple idea came to Mia in that moment.

Activating a small sigil on her left hand, Mia started the simplest spell she could think of. It was a spell Mia had added to her arsenal to use on *herself*. This wouldn't normally work in a fight. Hell, this *shouldn't* work in a fight. This was not remotely how this spell was supposed to be used.

But hell, it was worth a shot.

Mia charged Mark, pressing her hand to his chest. At first he looked shocked, his eyes going wide for a moment before rolling back in his head. His knees then buckled, and Mia caught him, guiding him down slowly as he collapsed onto the porch completely unconscious.

"Well he's flat on his ass. How did you do that?"

Mia looked up to see Riley standing in the door.

"It's literally just a spell I use when I'm having trouble with my insomnia," Mia said, grabbing her jacket off of the wooden decking of the porch. "It really shouldn't have worked. That spell is like literally the easiest thing to block if you want to."

"What do we do now," Riley sighed, putting her hand on her hip.

"Tie him up and board up the broken window?" Mia said with a shrug. "And then we better come up with a plan fast for when he wakes up."

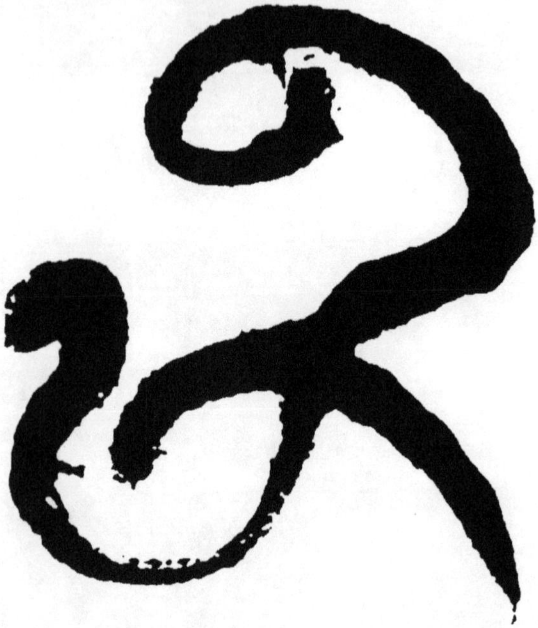

Chapter 14

"It's been a while since you knocked him out, when do you think he's going to wake up?" Riley asked, shifting her weight from foot to foot.

"The spell's designed to keep a person asleep for at least four hours, it's been three and a half," Mia sighed, sitting down on the drop cloth covered couch. Riley's living room was mid-renovation, and the floor was covered in sheets of plastic and canvas.

In the center of the space, Mark Durante was slumped in a chair, his wrists bound to its arms. On the floor around him were a hastily drawn set of sigils and runes.

Mia hoped they were enough to keep this thing contained.

"I got the window boarded up," Bobbi sighed, entering the room. "What's the plan?"

"It's pretty clear Mark's in the middle of being consumed by the true shadow," Mia said, leaning back into the couch. "We need to get it to let go. I don't have the power to remove it on my own."

"Then how do we save him?" Riley asked, pacing around the room.

"I need to cut him off from magic," Mia said. "But I can only pull that off if I can get Mark's consent to do it, and I don't feel like that's going to be easy."

"So when he wakes up we need to convince him to let you save him *and* get him to tell us Lisa's plan," Riley sighed, stopping by the large fireplace.

"Yeah, that's going to be a tough sell," Bobbi said, shaking her head.

"Don't really have any other options," Mia replied.

The three sat in tense silence as they waited for Mark to wake up from his mystically induced slumber. After just under a half an hour, his eyes began to open.

Mark looked gaunt and pale, his eyes appearing to sink back further in his head than normal. He looked up at Mia and tried to fight against his bonds.

"Mark, I need you to calm down," Mia said, getting up from the couch and crossing the room. "You need to listen to me very closely."

"I don't need to do anything," Mark replied, swirls of darkness dancing around his fingers. "You need to get out of my way."

"You're bound in pretty tight, don't waste your energy," Mia sighed. "You need to be saving every ounce you have if you're going to live, Mark."

"I don't believe you," Mark hissed.

"Yeah, I get that," Mia said, rubbing the back of her neck, trying to ignore how much the sigil there was burning. "But I don't know if you've looked in the mirror lately — because things aren't going that well. There is something inside you, something that is literally feeding on your life force as we speak."

Mark just stared at her silently.

"Okay, so this is what we need to do," Mia explained. "I need to sever you from magic. The shadow is using it to feed off of you, and if you're disconnected from it, the shadow can't anymore. This will only work if you let me though. I can only do it if you fully consent."

"I can't let you do that," Mark said, his eyes seemingly on fire. "Lisa needs me. We need to complete the plan."

"What is the plan, Mark," Riley chimed in. "What is it you all plan on doing?"

"You wouldn't understand," Mark spat. "What we're doing is righteous."

"You killed Greg and you're going after his dad," Bobbi said, stepping forward. "And Mark, I know that what they did to Lisa was awful, but this isn't the way to get it done. This will kill Lisa too."

"What do you care about what happens to Lisa?" Mark said, craning his head to look at Bobbi. "You're no better than the Van Burens, using people like they were nothing."

Roils of shadow began to swirl around Mark like a storm, pushing against the wards that kept him contained.

"Mark, I need you to focus," Mia said, trying to get things back on track. "You need to stop trying to break free and let me help you."

"Help me?" Mark laughed. "You couldn't help me if you tried. We're going to remove any trace of Thomas Van Buren, and when we're done we're going to turn our eyes on you."

"How are you going to remove any trace of him," Riley interjected, crossing her arms.

"We're going to do to him what we tried and failed to do to the first time to Greg," Mark said with a grin. "If you think what happened to him was bad, just wait until you see what happens to his dad. Of course, when we succeed, you won't remember *anything*, so what does it matter."

Mark began to quietly laugh to himself.

"Mark, you need to stop right now," Mia said. There wasn't much time left, and it was clear that he was pushing against the wards as hard as he could. Mia wasn't sure how long they would hold, and she likely could only protect just herself if Mark got free. "Bobbi, Riley… why don't you two leave the room."

"We can help Mia," Bobbi replied.

"Bobbi, no," Riley saw the look in Mia's eyes and began to put things together. "We should leave Mia alone. Let her talk to Mark on her own."

"I don't—" Bobbi started.

"Hit the showers, Crawford," Mia said, hoping Riley and Bobbi would get the hint to head to the nearest warded area of the house.

"Trust me," Riley said, guiding Bobbi out of the room and towards the stairs. "Mia can handle this."

As Riley and Bobbi exited, Mia could see the wards restraining Mark beginning to falter. She quietly reactivated her own personal protections, hoping he didn't notice.

"I know you don't believe me, but where do you think that power you're using is coming from, Mark?" Mia said slowly. "Like I said before, that thing inside you is feeding on your life force and your soul. You're literally burning yourself away every time you use it, and you're going to die if you don't stop now."

"Liar!" Mark yelled, the blackness swirling around him almost made it hard to make out his face now. "You're nothing but a liar, and I refuse to believe anything that you say!"

He was pushing hard, and using so much power Mia knew the binding wards holding him in place were about to fail. She had to get him to stop.

"Mark, please. I'm begging you to calm—"

The wards around Mark shattered like ethereal glass, sending shards of energy across the room. Mia managed to brace herself just in time to prevent being knocked over.

"You are not the one who's in control here, I am!" Mark screamed. Pure darkness surrounded him, moving like an endless storm. "You can't stop me!"

"Mark, I—" Mia tried to speak, but tendrils of shadow exploded from Mark and tossed her across the room, slamming her into the wall.

The impact knocked the breath out of Mia as she slumped against the wall, feeling the familiar sting of pain coursing through her body. Her wards could keep the tendrils from literally touching her, but not the pressure wave that came with them.

She struggled to regain her footing, her vision swimming from the force of the blow.

Mark, consumed by the shadow's influence, advanced towards her with terrifying certainty. His eyes glowed with an otherworldly gleam that sent shivers down Mia's spine. The room seemed to grow colder, the air thick with malevolent energy.

"You should have listened, Mia," Mark's voice echoed like a haunting whisper. "Now it's too late for you to stop me."

"You don't understand, Mark," Mia said, catching her breath. "I don't need to stop you. Every action you take brings you closer to nonexistence. I'm literally trying to save your life, you moron."

Mark lunged at her, the darkness surrounding him writhing and twisting like snakes. Mia's heart pounded in her chest as she braced herself, her magic clashing against the shadow's invading energy.

"Mark, you have to understand!" Mia shouted, her voice trembling. "You're only making it worse. You're destroying yourself for nothing!"

The darkness seethed around him, the air crackling with static electricity. The shadows reached towards her, clawing at the air as if trying to grab hold of Mia's essence. She could feel the power of the shadow pressing against her wards, threatening to break through at any moment.

"You can't stop me," Mark growled, his voice taking on a menacing, echoing quality. "I won't fall for your lies and deceit."

Mark couldn't see how his own body was wasting away in front of Mia's eyes. With every attack, he appeared gaunter and gaunter. He wasn't going to last long, and Mia knew there wasn't anything she could do now.

But she couldn't stop trying.

"Mark, this is it. This is where it ends," Mia said, trying to catch her breath. "If you stop now, I might still be able to save you. But this is your last chance."

"Stop lying to m—" Mark stopped, finally glancing at his hands. His skin was ashen white and his hands appeared almost skeletal. "What's… what's happening to me… what did you do to me!"

"I've been trying to warn you," Mia answered. "It's eating you alive, and only you can stop it. Please stop."

"No! You're a liar!" Mark roared. He pushed forward, one last burst of darkness smashed into Mia, slamming her against the wall. But as he did so, the last light faded from Mark's eyes. He seemed to freeze mid lunge, his face a morbid mask of rage.

Mia didn't move, taking in what had just happened. The buzzing on in the sigil on Mia's neck seemed to stop as the shadow retreated, leaving Riley's house, moving towards its next victim. As Mia stepped forward, the vibration in the floor was just enough to send what was left of Mark Durante crumbling into dust on the floor.

"God damn it, kid," Mia sighed, crouching down to the pile of dust and debris that had once been Mark. "Why wouldn't you let me save you."

Chapter 15

The winter wind picked up and seemed to howl and whine at the old windows of the Rose House. A cold draft whipped through the room, and Mia wasn't sure if it was the winter worming its way through the cracks of the old home or the spirits that filled its halls.

"So is it over?" Riley's voice called from the hallway. "Because it sure got quiet down there."

"Yeah!" Mia called back, collapsing on the couch. "Kind of the worst outcome, but its over."

"You're still alive, so I wouldn't call it the *worst* outcome," Riley said, re-entering the living room. Bobbi was close behind and visibly exhausted.

"So he didn't make it, huh," Bobbi said, looking at the pile of ash that had once been Mark Durante. "God damn it."

"Took the words right out of my mouth," Mia sighed. She felt like crumpling into a ball at the moment. Her battle with Mark and the shadow had drained her of most of her fight. "I feel like absolute trash right now."

"Drinks, we need drinks," Riley said. "I'll be right back."

Bobbi pulled a canvas sheet off of a large arm chair, and sat down in it as Riley exited the room. After a few moments, Riley returned with a bottle of whiskey and sat down on the couch next to Mia.

"I could have saved him if he'd let me," Mia sighed, taking the bottle from Riley. "Why wouldn't he let me save him."

"Because he's Mark, and he already didn't trust you," Bobbi answered, even though she clearly knew Mia wasn't looking for an answer. "Add in that shadow thing, and there was zero chance he'd turn things around."

"Maybe you're right," Mia said, taking a swig from the bottle. "I just wish I could do more."

"Is there a way to save them without their permission?" Bobbi asked earnestly. "Like I get that consent is important, but if it could keep them from dying?"

"It's not that simple," Mia said, taking another drink before handing the bottle back to Riley. "The amount of work a ritual like that would take is kind of incredible. Severing someone from magic against their will is not exactly easy."

"I assume we're talking about the same kind of power you had to use with the Mason Blackwood banishment?" Riley asked.

"Like that scale, but for multiple days on end," Mia sighed. "And we'd need more than just me. It's not impossible, but I don't think we have the time."

"So yeah, we need them to let us," Bobbi said dejectedly.

"It just sucks knowing you can try your hardest and not save anyone," Mia said shaking her head.

"At least you tried," Bobbi said, curling up in the chair. "And no matter what, we have to try."

"Do we?" asked Riley, a puzzled look on her face. "I mean, do we really need to keep trying?"

Mia looked over to Riley confused. "Yeah, Riley — we do. Why wouldn't we keep going?"

"Because they're murderers?" Riley said, blinking. "Look, these people murdered someone in cold blood. Now, I don't want them to die, but you've told them what will happen. Like, you did your part? At this point, it feels like they're getting what they deserve."

"What they 'deserve?'" Mia said incredulously. "Did you really just say that?"

"I mean, you can show someone the danger they're in, but if they choose to ignore it, what can you do?" Riley asked, taking a sip from the bottle of whiskey. "And frankly, for people who seem to have no remorse for killing someone, I don't think there's any coming back for them to begin with."

Mia sat for a second, looking at the ground. "You think there's no coming back?"

"From killing someone?" Riley replied. "No, I don't think there is."

"Like obviously they aren't remorseful *right now*, but you don't think there's any chance for them?" Bobbi asked, looking shocked.

"Not really?" Riley said. "I mean, once you cross that line you can't really come back."

"Riley," Mia said, still looking down. "I've killed before, you know that, right?"

"I mean yeah," Riley shrugged. "But those were vampires. It was a whole thing. Exigent circumstances."

"No, Riley," Mia said, looking up finally. "I've killed someone with magic before. Like a normal person."

Riley paused for a moment, a look of shock forming on her face. "But they were some other witch or something, and it was them or you…"

"No, just a normal person," Mia said, shaking her head. "I was… you know things weren't always so easy for me. I've told you that Sarah and I were barely surviving at one point."

Riley just stared back silently.

"We found our first bit of luck when I got a job as a waitress, getting paid under the table, but Sarah…" Mia took a moment. "Sarah wasn't doing stuff that was strictly legal. She ended up doing odd jobs for this guy… let's call him Jack."

Explaining this was hard. It was never easy to talk about this part of her past, but Mia knew she needed Riley to hear it.

"This guy, he was a real dirtbag. He tried to take advantage of her, kept pressuring her to…" Mia kept her eyes on Riley, hoping Riley might understand. "He kept escalating. She quit almost immediately, but he kept after her. He'd find where we were staying and circle the block in his car sometimes."

"Why didn't you just go to the police?" Riley asked, folding her arms. She was tense, almost like a closed fist.

"And tell them what?" Mia replied. "We both had rap sheets at that point, and we couldn't risk me losing my job too. Hell, Jack kept saying that if Sarah didn't do what he wanted, *he'd* call the cops and claim we stole something from him."

This was the part Mia hated saying the most. This was the part where she needed to admit what she did.

"We didn't have anywhere to turn. He was relentless, and it went on for months. We never felt safe," Mia sighed. "I decided I would take things into my own hands. I was just trying to drive him away, but I was new to magic. I… I ended up blowing up his car with him inside."

"Jesus, Mia…" Riley whispered.

"I didn't mean to, and I wouldn't do it again — but I don't regret it," Mia said, locking eyes with Riley. "It saved our lives. Some days even I find myself wishing I'd done it sooner."

"It's not the same, you didn't have options," Riley replied.

"Isn't it?" Bobbi asked. "I mean, Lisa felt helpless, and Greg's dad is incredibly powerful. What options did she have."

"And if there's no way to save these kids, or for them to find redemption, then how could there possibly be for me?" Mia asked.

"It's different!" Riley said, getting up from the couch. "You were homeless and living on the streets, these are a bunch of privileged college kids! It's just... it's just not the same."

"I think you're wrong," Mia said quietly. "I think it's exactly the same."

"I'm not listening to this," Riley said dismissively. "It's late, and I need sleep. I'm going to bed. I don't know if you're staying here or at your place tonight, Mia, but do what you want."

Riley walked out of the room, and stomped up the stairs.

"So... uh... *that* went well," Bobbi said, still curled up in the chair.

"Which part, the bit where I failed saving Mark, or the part where Riley stormed off in a huff?" Mia asked, her voice filled with exhaustion.

"Both," Bobbi said. "I only wish Riley hadn't taken the whiskey with her."

"Yeah, that kind of sucks," Mia sighed. "I'd really like to be drunk right now."

"Mia, I think I need to tell Lisa about what happened to Mark," Bobbi said, shifting in her chair. "She deserves to know what happened to her friend."

"You know you can't do that, Bobbi," Mia said, lying back on the couch. "She's not going to believe you, and she might hurt you."

"I know, it's a massive risk," Bobbi nodded. "But I need to tell her."

"I get where you're coming from, I really do. But Lisa is not remotely stable right now," Mia said, sitting up and fixing her gaze on Bobbi. "Telling her about Mark could set off a chain of events we might not be able to control."

Bobbi hesitated, her expression torn between loyalty to Mark and the need to protect herself. "I know, Mia, but I can't just sit back and do nothing. Mark was one of her best friends. She deserves to know."

"She's going to blame us, blame *you* for it," Mia said. "That could be so dangerous."

"And that's a risk I may need to take," Bobbi replied. "Sometimes doing the right thing isn't the same as doing the safe thing."

Mia thought for a moment, brushing a few dark curls out of her face.

"You really care for her, don't you," Mia said quietly. "God, you've fallen for her hard."

"I don't know," Bobbi said, shifting uncomfortably.

"Yeah, yeah you have," Mia said, a sad smile forming on her face. "Oh Bobbi, you really know how to pick them."

"I just like being around her," Bobbi replied. "I just wish she still liked being around me."

"Yeah, we kind of blew that up for you," Mia said. "I really am sorry we got you involved in this. You should have never been put in that position."

"I made my own choices, Mia," Bobbi looked at Mia and shook her head. "I'm not some child that needs to be coddled."

"I know, Bobbi. I know," Mia got up off the couch and stood at the center of the room. "But you still can't go tell Lisa about Mark. I need to know that you understand that."

"I understand, you don't want me to go tell Lisa," Bobbi nodded.

"I'm not kidding, Bobbi. I need you to promise me you're not going to go tell her," Mia pleaded.

"I get it. I promise," Bobbi responded.

"You promise that you're not going to tell Lisa," Mia said, narrowing her eyes.

"I promise I won't tell Lisa," Bobbi said with a nod.

"You swear?" Mia asked.

"I swear."

Chapter 16

Bobbi moved quietly down the stairs, trying her best not to let the boards creak as she moved through the darkened Rose House. As she slipped on her jacket and boots, Bobbi could hear Mia snoring from where she'd gone to sleep on Riley's living room couch. Whenever Mia used that much magic at once she usually crashed pretty hard afterwards, so there wasn't much risk of waking her up.

She really had meant it when she promised Mia she wouldn't go, but it had been gnawing at her all night. She just couldn't sleep with the knowledge that Mark was dead and no one knew. Lisa might not be happy to see her, and it might even put Bobbi in danger just to show her face. But it was the right thing to do, and if her father had taught her anything it was that sometimes you had to do the right thing even if it wasn't easy.

Well, that and how to field dress a deer in under five minutes. He definitely taught her how to do that too.

Bobbi stepped out into the cold winter night, pulling up her hood as a buffer to the wind. She'd left her truck parked back by Mia's store, and it was going to be a long walk back to campus.

The streets of Parrish Mills were eerily quiet as Bobbi crunched through the snow covered sidewalks. It was only ten thirty at night, but this far away from campus the town had already fully gone to sleep. The peaceful quiet left her alone with her thoughts, and it reminded her of being out alone in the woods growing up.

Bobbi would much rather be in the woods right now.

Eventually she made it to campus and headed towards the library. Lisa had posted something about studying late there, and had forgotten to block all of Bobbi's accounts. Hopefully the public setting would keep things civil.

Hopefully.

The problem with knowing someone is in the library is that it's very different than knowing *where* in the library they are. Bobbi found herself walking through the endless stacks and study carrels scanning for Lisa's face. The Garrity University library was huge, and it was like looking for a needle in a haystack even this late at night.

Eventually she made it up to the third floor, where the research texts were far more obscure and specialized than the lower levels. You could hear a pin drop up here, and every step Bobbi made on carpet felt like a cacophonous thud. Bobbi's head snapped to the right when the sound of a turning page caught her attention.

There she was, Lisa Farris. Seated at a table in the corner. No turning back now.

Bobbi steeled herself and began her approach. When she was steps away, Lisa looked up and practically jumped out of her chair in shock. Lisa's expression turned from surprise to furrowed anger rather quickly though, as she leaned back and folded her arms.

"What do you want, Bobbi," Lisa said in hushed tones. While it was likely they were the only ones on the third floor, there was always a chance they weren't and Lisa wouldn't want to be overheard.

Bobbi grabbed another chair at the table and sat down, readying herself to deliver the worst news she could think of.

"Lisa, I need to tell you something," Bobbi said, trying to breathe slowly.

"Are you here to say you're sorry?" Lisa spat. "That you didn't mean to manipulate me into bed? And then immediately go tell your friend about it?"

"That's not... I mean I *am* sorry," Bobbi shook her head. "And I know I fucked up, but I *really* do like you. I wasn't faking that."

"Bullshit," Lisa sneered. "I'm not accepting whatever bullshit apology you're here to deliver so you can sleep better at night. You don't get absolution from me tonight."

"I wouldn't expect it," Bobbi said, trying to figure out the best way to tell Lisa. "What I did is unforgivable. I never should have slept with you. It's... it's not why I'm here either."

"Then spit it out," Lisa replied, leaning back in her chair. "What is so important that you stalked me here for? What could you possibly have to say?"

"Mark's dead," Bobbi blurted out, bracing herself for what might come next.

"What do you mean 'Mark's dead?'" Lisa said, her face dropping. "I just saw him earlier today. What are you talking about."

"Mark came to where I've been staying right now, and he attacked Mia," Bobbi said slowly. "They fought, but he started to use these... shadows? Like black shadowy stuff started coming out of him."

Lisa just sat there, staring at Bobbi. Silently judging her as Bobbi desperately tried to explain.

"The shadows... they were draining the life out of him," Bobbi said, trying not to tear up. "Mia begged him to let her help him, but he refused to let her. It… it consumed him Lisa. There was nothing left of him. He was just gone."

Lisa took a moment and steadied herself against the table. After a few minutes, she spoke. "Did you see this yourself."

"No," Bobbi shook her head. "At that point I was hiding in another room."

"So Mia told you that this is what happened?" Lisa asked, raising an eyebrow.

"Yeah, I mean, she's the one who was there," Bobbi shrugged. "I'm so sorry Lisa."

Lisa paused for a moment, examining Bobbi's face.

"Oh god, you really believe her, don't you," Lisa said with a sigh. "You think Mia's telling you the truth."

"What?"

"Bobbi, Mia's lying to you," Lisa said shaking her head. "She killed Mark, and she's covering it up to make it seem like she wasn't the bad guy. And you've bought into it, like hook, line, and sinker."

"She's not — Mia's not lying, Lisa," Bobbi insisted. "The true shadow destroyed Mark, and if you're not careful it's going to come after you too."

"God, she really has you brainwashed," Lisa said, her eyes wide. "She's a manipulator who's afraid of anyone who challenges her power or doesn't fall in line with how she thinks you should act. You need to snap out of it, Bobbi."

"I'm not… that isn't what's happening, Lisa," Bobbi said, looking Lisa dead in the eye. "There is a thing that is coming for you and your friends, and Mia's your only chance at surviving it."

"God, this is just sad," Lisa sat back in her chair. "You've just bought all of her lies yourself. That's why you're so loyal. It kind of makes me feel *bad* for you."

"You need to believe me, Lisa," Bobbi said, leaning forward. "This is important."

"I know you think it is," Lisa sighed. "God, you fully drank Mia's Kool Aid. I appreciate you telling me about Mark, but I can handle myself. Mia Graves will pay for what she's done, and you might want to steer clear."

"Lisa that's not what's happening," Bobbi argued. "You've got it wrong."

"You need to leave now, Bobbi," Lisa said quietly. "I really need you to go."

"Lisa…"

"Go, Bobbi," Lisa snarled, her blue eyes as cold as ice.

Bobbi stood and headed towards the stairs. She could feel Lisa's eyes on her until the stairwell door clicked closed behind her. Doing the right thing wasn't always easy, and sometimes it could make things worse.

As she left the building, Bobbi began to slowly walk back to Riley's house. It was cold, it was windy, and things seemed bleaker than ever.

As she stepped back in to the Rose House, Bobbi leaned dejectedly against the wall as she pried off her boots.

"So where were you?" asked Riley from down the hall.

"You're up?" Bobbi asked, taking off her coat.

"Yeah, didn't really go to bed," Riley shrugged. "I've just been doom scrolling in my room for hours and figured I'd come down now that Mia's asleep. Still avoiding my question though."

"I went to tell Lisa what happened to Mark," Bobbi said. "She deserved to know."

"Maybe," Riley said, approaching Bobbi. "But that was still dumb as hell."

"Yeah, probably," Bobbi said with a small grin. "But we all know I do dumb things."

Bobbi walked into the living room and sat down in the arm chair she'd occupied earlier that night. Mia was flopped across the couch like a sleeping cat on her back, her mouth hanging open. Her snoring provided a slow a gentle roar.

"God, she can sleep through anything," Riley shook her head. "You know, when I stayed with her when we first met she complained about how much *I* snored…"

"…but I'm betting you didn't randomly yell stuff out like 'Sarah, get back in the car!' at three in the morning," Bobbi laughed.

"Oh my god, she talks in her sleep *so much*," Riley said with a smile. "One night she went on for twenty minutes rattling off answers to questions about a diner menu that literally no one asked. I've never needed that much information about a patty melt."

"No! Help me with the door, Sarah!" Mia yelled out as if on queue, before turning on her side. Bobbi and Riley both started laughing.

"God, this is the woman we rely on to save us," Riley said, rolling her eyes. "Like this is literally the most capable person I know."

"I think I fucked up, Riley," Bobbi said, shifting in her chair. "Lisa thinks Mia killed Mark on purpose."

"Well that's not good," Riley replied, her eyes wide.

"Yeah, no, it's really bad," Bobbi said, her eyes on the floor. "I tried to explain to her what actually happened, but she's convinced Mia has it out for her."

"You can't make someone believe something they don't want to, Bobbi," Riley sat down in a chair across from Bobbi, still covered in a sheet. "You know that's not how people work."

"I know," Bobbi said, curling into a ball in her chair. "But I really don't want things to get worse. I just want…"

"You like her, and you want to save her," Riley sighed. "But maybe that's not the foundation for a healthy relationship."

"No Sarah, we save each other," Mia half muttered, her leg twitching. "Isswha we do."

Bobbi raised a hand and pointed at Mia.

"Oh my god no," Riley laughed. "You are not holding up Mia and Sarah as an example. They've spent the last couple years running away from each other after Sarah literally lost *half of her soul*."

"I dunno, it's a bit romantic," Bobbi shrugged.

"First off, no — it's fucked up is what it is," Riley said, folding her arms. "Secondly, I don't have time to unpack how weird it is that you're romanticizing the relationship between the woman you've been hooking up with and her ex-girlfriend."

"I'm complicated," Bobbi said, still folded into the chair.

"Only as complicated as you choose to be," Riley sighed. A look of exasperation crossed her face. "God, who am I to talk. Last guy I dated was an undead mass murderer."

"Everything is terrible," Bobbi muttered, seemingly shrinking even smaller in the chair.

"Yeah, but at least we can still get drunk."

Chapter 17

"Were you followed?" Lisa asked, her voice low and steady.

"No," Alexis shook her head, shaking the snow off her boots. "I-I wasn't."

"It's not like they don't know where I live," Theresa said, entering the living room. "Like if they wanted to figure out where we were going, they could just swing by."

"Still, we can't be too careful," Lisa said, shaking her head. The run down college house Theresa lived in was in a perpetual state of mess, but it seemed even worse than normal. Empty cans and old pizza boxes littered every spare surface, and the general miasma of filth seemed to occupy every corner of the space.

That wasn't even mentioning the *smell*.

But the house gave them space to work, and they couldn't really do that back on campus. They needed privacy.

"None of my roommates are home," Theresa said, clearing some space off of one of the couches and sitting down. "We should have the place to ourselves for the next few hours."

"Good, we need to talk about some stuff," Lisa said, bracing herself. "I need to tell you guys something, and it might be hard to hear."

She took a deep breath. It wouldn't help to beat around the bush, and it definitely wouldn't make it easier to say. Alexis and Theresa needed to hear this, and they needed to hear it now.

"Mark's dead," Lisa said quietly.

A stunned silence took the room. Lisa paused, searching their faces for a reaction. Alexis's eyes widened in shock, her hands trembling slightly. Theresa let out a soft gasp, her pink-dyed hair falling like a curtain around her face. The weight of Lisa's words hung heavy in the air, suffocating them all.

"How?" Alexis finally managed to croak out, her voice barely above a whisper.

"Mia killed him," Lisa answered.

"What?" Theresa said, standing back up.

"I don't… I don't understand," Alexis said, clearly in a state of shock. "W-why would Mia do that?"

"Mark did something stupid," Lisa replied, looking down towards her feet. "He was pissed yesterday, and went after her on his own. I don't know exactly what happened, but Bobbi told me there was a fight — and Mark didn't make it out alive."

"You spoke to Bobbi?" Theresa asked, raising an eyebrow. "After everything she did?"

"She found me in the library last night to tell me," Lisa said. "I may be pissed at her, but it was the decent thing to do."

"So it was self defense," Alexis said quietly. "Mia only killed him because he attacked her."

"I don't know for sure, but maybe," Lisa said, looking up through her long, dark hair. "But it means Mia might know what we're planning, which means if we're going to get it done, we need to move fast."

"Are you… are you sure you still want to go through with it?" Theresa said, putting her hand on Lisa's shoulder.

"Mark died trying to keep the plan on track," Lisa said, looking up at Theresa. "I'm not going to let that be in vain. We need to get to work. We need to get back on track *now*."

"Okay, so I've been trying to figure out where we went wrong the last time," Alexis said, pushing trash off of a coffee table. She pulled a notebook out of her backpack and opened it, displaying it as best she could on the table's stained surface. "When we cast the spell on Greg, I think we set the sigils too close in proximity to where he was standing. I think the spell would have worked as intended if we'd spaced them out about ten times further apart."

It always amazed Lisa how Alexis could switch from quiet and nervous to the chattiest person you've ever met when she got onto a topic she really cared about.

"Now targeting State Senator Van Buren is going to be harder than targeting Greg was," Alexis continued, seemingly not even pausing to take breaths. "Greg was easy to lure to the park. We had a ton of time to integrate the sigils into the natural landscape, and we knew he wouldn't tell anyone where he was going ahead of time. While we know where Greg's dad is thanks to the tracking spell Mark put on him at the vigil, we can't exactly maneuver him into a specific position of our choice. We'll have to go to him, but that means we won't be able to prep the space we cast the spell at."

"So what's the solution?" Lisa asked.

"We build the sigils portably," Alexis explained, pointing at some sketches in her notepad. "Rather than spending time building the sigils into a permanent location, we construct them individually as talismans. It means we'll have to cast each one of the spells individually first, but once we do we can set them up wherever we need to."

"With Mark... gone... how do you propose we execute the final spell?" Theresa said, looking over the notebooks on the table. "We've always worked with the full four of us — only having three changes things."

"I don't think it changes it that much," Alexis said, cleaning off her glasses. "If I modify the sigils a bit, we should be able to easily adapt it to a three point instead of four point configuration."

"That's pretty impressive, Alexis," Lisa said with a small smile. "When did you have time to come up with this?"

"I've been working on the portabilization options for the last week or so," Alexis said. "The three person variation I added yesterday... because I was thinking about stepping back. I didn't want you to have to stop just because I was... because I was too afraid."

"You're not afraid now?" Lisa asked.

"Mark's dead now," Alexis replied. "You need me now."

"Hey, we *always* need you," Theresa said.

"Yeah, Alexis, we never could have gotten this far without you," Lisa said. "Frankly I don't know what I would do if you weren't here."

Lisa was good at a lot of things, but Alexis operated on a level that sometimes astonished even her. Lisa felt like she had a solid grasp on magical theory, but Alexis seemed to be able to focus in on it in ways that were almost otherworldly on their own.

"So, if we're in a hurry, we should start with enchanting the base talismans," Alexis said, clearly trying to stay focused. "I brought some materials we can use to construct them, and then we can perform the necessary rituals to effectively pre-engage them."

"Hell yeah, Alexis with the arts and crafts to save the day," Theresa nodded. "What are we using to make these?"

"The spell says they have to be natural materials... so I've got wood and clay," Alexis started pulling materials out of her bag. "We can carve into the wood for two, and shape clay into what we need for the earthen ones. Afterwards we can bake the clay in your oven."

"Let's get started then," Lisa said, glancing between Alexis and Theresa. "We'll make the physical talismans, and then perform the ritual to empower them."

The three young women got to work immediately, the urgency of the situation palpable in the air. Alexis meticulously carved intricate runes into the wooden talismans, her hands steady as she poured her focus into each stroke. Theresa worked on shaping the clay with a deft touch, forming it into the needed symbols for their spell. The room filled with the earthy scent of clay and the sharp tang of freshly carved wood.

Lisa watched them both, her heart heavy with the weight of their mission and the loss of Mark. She couldn't afford to dwell on grief now; they had to move forward, for Mark's sake, for their own sake.

As Alexis finished carving the last rune on the piece of wood she was crafting, she glanced up at Lisa and Theresa. "So it will probably take forty minutes to bake the clay ones. The instructions are on the slip I put on the table."

"On it!" Theresa said, grabbing the slip and taking the talismans into the kitchen.

"So you're sure about what went wrong?" Lisa said, sitting down on the couch. "I don't think I'd feel bad if we accidentally burned the state senator alive too, but it's still not what I want."

"I'm pretty sure?" Alexis said. "I mean, Iggatol was a bit vague on this one, and removing a person from the memory of all living beings is incredibly hard."

"So they're baking!" Theresa announced, reentering the room. "We could probably do the ritual in here if we move the furniture, but the basement is always available if we move Kev's drum kit."

"I am not touching Kev's stuff again," Lisa replied. "Theresa, you and I should start moving stuff out of the way, while Alexis can set up the materials for the ritual."

"Cool cool," Theresa nodded. "Grab the other side of this couch?"

As Lisa and Theresa began to move the furniture, a sudden chill filled the room. The air seemed to thicken with an oppressive darkness that made the hairs on their arms stand on end. Alexis looked up from her work, a frown creasing her brow as she scanned the space.

"Did you guys feel that?" Alexis asked, her voice barely above a whisper.

"Probably just a draft," Theresa shrugged. "This house is old as fuck, and this time of year stuff gets randomly cold. The upstairs is like ten degrees warmer than it is down here."

By the time the three had the living room in its perfect arrangement and all of the spell components in place, the timer on the oven went off.

"Okay, do not touch these things under any circumstances," Theresa said, retrieving the clay talismans. "They are hot as all get out."

"We can still cast the ritual on them," Alexis replied. "But yeah, don't touch them unless you want massive burns."

"Alexis, you're the one who figured out the modified three person version of the ritual, so you should lead it," Lisa said quietly.

"Really?" Alexis asked nervously. "Are you sure?"

"Yeah," Lisa answered. "I think you're ready."

Alexis took a deep breath, steeling herself for what was to come. She positioned the talismans in a precise pattern on the coffee table, their surfaces still radiating heat from the oven. The sense of foreboding in the room seemed to intensify, as if the air itself was holding its breath in anticipation.

Theresa and Lisa stood on either side of Alexis, their eyes fixed on her as she began to recite the incantation. Her voice was steady, each word resonating with power and purpose. The room seemed to hum with magical energy, the sigils on the talismans glowing faintly in response to Alexis's words.

As the ritual reached its crescendo, a sudden gust of wind swept through the room, causing the candles to flicker wildly and casting eerie shadows on the walls. Alexis's voice wavered for a moment, but she quickly regained her composure, her will unwavering.

As they neared the completion of the spell, a sudden darkness took the room. It was gone in an instant, but left Lisa gasping and confused.

"What just happened?" Lisa choked out. The clay talismans were cracked and covered in frost, and Theresa lay on the ground shaking.

"I don't know!" Alexis replied in a panic, running to Theresa's side.

"What the actual fuck?" Theresa coughed as Alexis helped her to her feet. "Something just hit me like a freight train."

The room was filled with a heavy silence, broken only by Theresa's ragged breathing and the crackling of the frost-covered talismans. Lisa's heart raced in her chest as she surveyed the scene before her, a chill creeping up her spine.

"Was that us?" Lisa said, her voice tinged with fear.

"N-No... that wasn't us," Alexis responded, holding Theresa up. The air felt charged with a malevolent energy, like a storm waiting to break loose. "I d-don't know what the heck that was."

"God I feel weird," Theresa said, finding her footing. "Like I feel heavy right now. Do we want to keep going?"

"We can't," Lisa growled. "The clay talismans are destroyed, we'd have to start from scratch. And there's no guarantee this wouldn't happen again. Something... no, *someone* just attacked us."

"Who?" Theresa asked.

"I mean, it's pretty obvious," Lisa shook her head. "Who knows what techniques we're using and is actively trying to stop us?"

"You're not suggesting Mia did this?" Alexis said, her eyes wide. "She wouldn't outright go after us like this, would she?"

"She killed Mark!" Lisa snapped. "And now she's attacked Theresa."

Theresa's eyes widened in realization, her breathing shallow as she took in Lisa's accusation. The fear that coursed through Alexis was mirrored on her face, a mix of disbelief and unease painted across her features.

Lisa's anger simmered like a pot ready to boil over, her jaw clenching at the thought of Mia laughing at her. "I know you admire her, Alexis, but we can't ignore the signs. This was too convenient a disruption, too targeted."

Alexis hesitated, and Lisa could tell she was torn between her loyalty to Mia and the mounting evidence. "I... I don't want to believe it," she whispered, her voice barely audible in the charged atmosphere.

"I think Lisa's right," Theresa said, still unsteady on her feet. "I feel like something's got a hold of me. Like it's draining me and filling me with... something. She's the only witch in town strong enough to hit me with a spell like that."

"What... what do we do?" Alexis pleaded, looking to Lisa for answers. "Mark might have been self defense, but this was a straight attack."

"We stop playing nice," Lisa said with a snarl. "Grab every enchanted tool we've got and prep any spells you can. That woman is going to regret the day she decided to fuck with us. Van Buren can wait, we need to destroy Mia Graves."

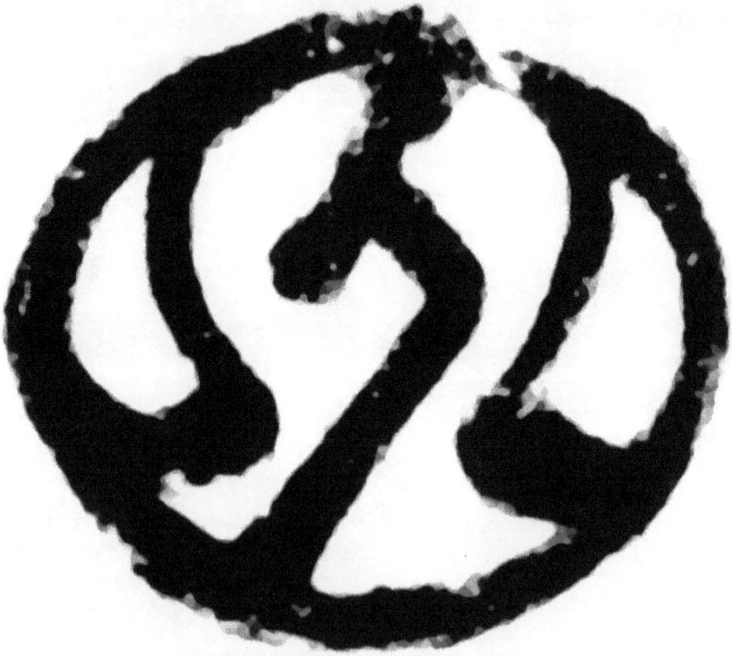

Chapter 18

"I'm just saying that the world's not so black and white, Riley," Mia shrugged, rifling through the kitchen cabinets of the Rose House. "Sometimes people don't feel like they have choices, and they'll do whatever it takes to survive. To condemn them for that seems extreme."

"Murder is murder, Mia," Riley replied, not looking up from her laptop. "And I guess maybe I don't feel bad when someone gets what's coming to them."

"So you'd be fine if we just let them die?" Mia asked, cocking her head. "You think that if someone kills their abuser they deserve the death penalty?"

"I'm not saying that Mia," Riley shook her head. "God, I am not saying that."

Riley let out a frustrated sigh and closed her laptop, finally turning to face Mia. The tone of their voices was light, but there as an underlying tension laced within as they stood on opposite sides of the kitchen, their gazes locked in a silent battle of wills.

"I just... I don't know, Mia," Riley began, her voice tinged with uncertainty. "I guess it's just hard for me to wrap my head around all of this. I'm used to a world where right and wrong actually seem to matter. Where *justice* matters."

Mia softened her expression, understanding the weight of their situation. She walked over to Riley and placed a comforting hand on her shoulder. "I get it, Riles. And I'm not defending them — I just don't want people to die because they made an understandable mistake."

Riley nodded. "It's just… you're trying to save someone who murdered a person and doesn't want your help. I don't know how hard you should try in these circumstances."

"I try because I feel like I've been that girl," Mia said, leaning against the counter. "People got hurt because of me, and if I can't help someone like Lisa come back from the edge, what hope is there for me?"

"I don't think I thought of it that way," Riley whispered.

"It's okay," Mia sighed, turning back to the kitchen cabinet. "Riley, why the hell do you have sixteen jars of peanut butter?"

"Normal reasons," Riley said, shifting her weight between her feet. "Perfectly normal reasons."

"There is no 'normal' reason to have this much peanut —" Mia stopped mid sentence as the visage of a twelve year old boy flickered into existence in the middle of the kitchen.

"Miss Riley! There's something urgent!" the specter spoke in a hurried tone.

"What is it Ben, another Amazon package?" Riley asked, sitting back down in her chair. Mia was still amazed at how used to living in a house full of ghosts Riley had gotten, because it sure spooked the hell out of Mia still.

"No miss, there are three women approaching the house," Ben said hurriedly. "And I think the same thing's wrong with one of them as that man from the other day."

"Shit," Riley said getting to her feet. "What do we do?"

"Bobbi's in the study, grab her and go to the upstairs bathroom," Mia said, snapping to attention. "I'll go deal with Nancy, Bonnie, and Rochelle."

"Who?"

"It's a movie, Riley," Mia said, making a beeline for the hallway to the foyer. "And yes I'm going to make you watch it some time."

Mia made it to the door, and contemplated putting on her jacket. Getting to her spells faster was probably going to be more important than keeping warm though, so she left it behind as she burst onto the front porch.

Standing in the front yard was Lisa, with Alexis and a pink haired young woman in stride. That must be Theresa.

And there was definitely something wrong with Theresa.

"Mia Graves!" Lisa bellowed, her eyes filled with anger. "I'm here to make you pay for what you've done."

"I don't know what you think I did, Lisa, but let's sit down and talk about this," Mia said, stepping forward on the porch. "There's no need to—"

A bolt of energy flew from Lisa's hand striking Mia in the shoulder, throwing her back through the air and smashing her into the side of the Rose House with a crack.

"Son of a..." Mia muttered, getting back to her feet. "Lisa, you need to—"

Another bolt flew from Lisa's hand, and Mia went to activate the shielding sigil on her right thigh through her jeans... and missed. The bolt struck Mia in the chest and knocked her down on her ass.

"Fucking hell," Mia grunted. Feeling her side, she was pretty certain that she'd just cracked a rib. Mia fumbled for the sigil on her leg a few more times before finding it. With the flick of a finger across the sigil, a wall of energy surrounded her. As she rose to her feet, a third bolt deflected off of the ward. "Lisa, you need to listen to me. You three are all in danger."

"Stop lying!" Lisa screamed. "The only danger has been you! You killed Mark, and then you came for the rest of us!"

"I didn't 'come for' anyone," Mia yelled back. God, even talking hurt right now. "And Mark was killed by the true shadow. It consumed him from the inside out! I tried to stop him! I tried to save him!"

"Liar!" Lisa yelled, striking Mia with another bolt. The source of the energy seemed to be coming from a set of bracelets around her wrists. Likely a a magical battery of some sort, which meant Lisa would likely run out of energy to keep attacking long before Mia's shields ran out.

But that didn't necessarily mean she had enough in reserve to deal with the other two. Mia needed to move to offense.

Mia's right hand danced across a set of sigils on her left forearm, and with a clap of her hands sent a shock wave of energy screaming across the front yard, knocking over Lisa and her cohorts.

With the touch of another sigil on her right arm, a torrent of wind picked up and pushed the three young witches down against the ground.

"You need to listen to me, Lisa, Alexis, Theresa…," Mia said slowly and calmly. "I did not kill Mark. I did not attack you. The magic you've been using is forbidden for a reason. It has drawn something called a true shadow to you, and since it's already found you, unless you let me sever you from magic, it *will* kill you."

"I don't believe you," Lisa replied. She tried to get off the ground, but was helpless against Mia's spell.

"Bullshit!" Theresa snapped, struggling against the cords of air that pinned her to the ground. "Just absolute bullshit!"

Theresa's eyes blackened, and she started to push herself off the ground, fighting against Mia's spell. Her skin grew paler, and tendrils of darkness began to dance around her fingers.

"Theresa… you need to stop that immediately," Mia said, moving carefully towards the pink haired young woman. "The more you touch the shadow, the faster it'll take you."

Theresa staggered to her feet, and unleashed a torrent of dark energy at Mia. Mia managed to stay upright, but found herself pushed across the ground. Lisa and Alexis looked on with horror as Theresa began to slowly transform before their eyes.

"God damn it stop, Theresa," Mia grunted, thankful her wards were holding as well as they were. "You're going to die if you keep doing this."

But Theresa seemed to ignore her, letting out a guttural roar as she struck at Mia again and again. Mia wasn't sure how long she could keep her wards working and keep Lisa and Alexis immobilized.

Mia had to make a choice.

With a snap of her fingers, Mia released the spell that was restraining Lisa and Alexis, refocusing the energy she had on hand at keeping Theresa's onslaught of attacks from touching her.

If the shadow directly touched her it could be *bad*.

Lisa and Alexis scrambled to their feet, watching in shock as Theresa continued her relentless assault on Mia. The air crackled with dark energy, and tendrils of shadow began to wrap around Theresa's arms like malevolent serpents.

Lisa stood in stunned silence, in shock from what she was witnessing.

"What's happening to her!" Alexis yelled.

"Like I tried to tell you, a true shadow is consuming her," Mia replied. "I wasn't... I wasn't ever lying to you about this."

"What do we do?" begged Alexis, looking at Theresa with a sense of absolute horror.

"Convince her to let me help her?" Mia grunted, as another wave of dark energy slammed into her. "I can only do it if she actually consents to it. If she fights me when I perform the ritual, it won't work!"

"Theresa! Please let her help you!" Alexis screamed.

Theresa turned her head slowly to face Alexis and narrowed her eyes.

"I don't... I don't want you to die, Theresa," Alexis pleaded. "Let her help you."

Theresa said one word, "Traitor."

Theresa unleashed a wave of shadows at Alexis. Mia tried to move as quickly as possible, activating a series of sigils to send something, *anything* to intercept that wave of shadow before it struck Alexis. The world almost seemed to slow to a crawl as a wave of white light streamed from Mia's hand and crossed between Alexis and Theresa's attack.

Mia's Hail Mary managed to absorb most of Theresa's attack, but a single tendril of shadow broke through and found purchase on Alexis's arm. Alexis screamed as shadowy tendril broke through her coat and burned her skin, leaving a blistering wound.

"What... what is happening," Lisa blinked tears from her eyes, her voice small and broken.

"Leave her alone, Theresa!" Mia said, running towards Alexis and checking her wounds. "You're not thinking straight — you need to stop now or else it's going to be too late."

"No! You're trying to trick me," Theresa yelled, turning her attention back to Mia. "You're trying to trick us all! You're trying to hurt Lisa!"

"She's not trying to trick us," Alexis gasped, grabbing her arm.

Theresa unleashed another attack against Mia, and Mia found herself tapping into her reserves to stop it. She was still only partially recovered from her fight with Mark, and deflecting the shadow's tendrils was taking more energy than anything she'd fought in her life. Mia wasn't sure how much longer she'd be able to keep going.

Lisa's eyes widened in horror as she saw the mark on Alexis's arm. She hesitated for a moment, unsure of what to do. But Mia's words echoed in her mind, and she knew she had to act.

"Theresa, what... what are you doing?" Lisa said, making her way to Alexis. "You attacked Beeds. Why would you attack Beeds?""

Theresa, her eyes now completely black, sneered at Lisa. "You're weak, Lisa. You don't understand what's at stake. We have to take control, we have to be strong!"

Roils of darkness swarmed her now gaunt features. She let out a primal scream as she sent wave after wave of darkness crashing into Mia's protective shields. Mia dug her heels into the snow covered lawn, just trying desperately to weather the storm.

Mia took a deep breath, her chest heaving with exhaustion. The sigils on her arms almost felt like they were burning, as she pulled every every ounce of reserve magic she had.

"I'm not the one doing this, Theresa," Mia shouted, her voice cracking under the strain. "Please stop now while there's still a chance to save you. Please!"

Lisa watched in horror as the darkness continued to worm its way into Theresa's body, her skin turning a sickly shade of ash. The once confident young woman looked almost broken as she stared in abject horror.

And then, as suddenly as it had begun, Theresa stopped, her face frozen in a terrifying rictus.

"Theresa?" Lisa asked, stepping towards the young woman's lifeless form. A wind blew through the trees, and Theresa's form crumbled to dust before them. "Oh god, oh my god... I was wrong... how could I have been so wrong..."

"Please, you have to listen to me," Mia begged. "I can save you but you have to let me. Please, I can't watch this happen again."

"Lisa? Mia? I don't feel good." Alexis said quietly. Still grasping her arm where Theresa's shadowy attack had struck her, Alexis collapsed on the ground.

Chapter 19

Mia and Lisa burst through the door of the Rose House as the two carried Alexis's limp form. The shadow was taking hold of her faster than Mia expected, and they didn't have much time.

"Riley! Bobbi! I need your help!" Mia yelled up the stairs. Mia and Lisa guided Alexis into the living room and laid her down on the ground.

"Alexis? Can you hear me?" Mia said, checking Alexis's pulse. It was still strong enough, the girl might still have a chance.

"Mia? I'm sorry I left work early without telling you the other day," Alexis muttered.

"Yeah, really not a priority right now, Alexis," Mia said quickly. "The shadow has a hold on you, and it's moving fast because of Theresa's attack. I need you to listen to me — I'm going to sever you from magic. It will stop the shadow from being able to feed on you, but I need your permission to do it."

"You have… you have my permission," Alexis whispered, her eyes filled with tears.

Bobbi ran into the room with Riley close behind.

"Oh shit," Bobbi said, looking around. "Where's Theresa?"

"She didn't make it," Mia replied. "Bobbi I need your help with this ritual. Riley, can you grab my bag from the kitchen?"

"On it it," Riley replied, bounding out of the room.

"What do you need me to do?" Bobbi asked.

"I'm wiped from what just happened outside, and I need a second person to add their energy to the spell," Mia said, pushing the furniture against the wall. "I know you've never done anything like this, but I mostly just need you to sit there and give me permission to draw from you."

"Can I help?" Lisa offered, desperation filling her eyes.

"No, no you can't," Mia responded while pulling up the rugs that covered Riley's living room floor. "Lisa, the shadow is coming for you too. Every time you touch magic, you light up like a beacon to that thing. Alexis is in worse shape right now, but you're not out of the woods either."

"Got your stuff!" Riley announced, bounding back into the room with Mia's brown satchel.

Mia grabbed some chalk out of her bag and started scrawling a complex set of sigils on the wooden floor. "Sorry about the floors, Riles."

"It's okay, I still need to refinish them in here anyways," Riley sighed.

"Bobbi, sit by Alexis's head on the edge of the circle," Mia said quickly while assembling a few other materials. "Alexis, I'm going to start now, are you ready?"

"Yes," Alexis replied, the word barely audible.

"Bobbi, I need you to place your hands on the edges of the circle I've drawn on the ground," Mia said, her hands moving carefully. "That way I can draw energy from you if I need to."

"On it," Bobbi nodded, placing her hands on the quickly drawn chalk lines on the floor.

"Riley? Lisa? I need you to stay back for now," Mia said as she began to work the ritual to sever Alexis from magic.

As Mia chanted the incantation, a soft glow enveloped Alexis, casting eerie shadows against the walls of the living room. Bobbi's eyes opened wide with surprise. She was likely feeling the draw of power through her body for the first time, and in a way Mia envied that experience.

The air crackled with magic, and a chorus of whispers filled the room, almost drowning out Mia's powerful voice.

As Mia's chanting reached a crescendo, Alexis let out a pained cry, her body arching off of the wooden floor. The shadows seemed to swirl around her, resisting Mia's efforts to sever the connection. But Mia was relentless, pouring everything she had into the ritual.

Suddenly, a blinding light erupted from Alexis, and a sickening pop cracked in the air.

The room fell to silence as the blinding light faded, leaving a sense of foreboding hanging in the air. Mia's heart raced as she watched Alexis lying motionless on the ground, unsure if she had successfully severed her from magic or if something had gone terribly wrong.

Bobbi stood frozen, her hands still resting on the chalk lines, a mix of fear and wonder in her eyes. Riley and Lisa exchanged a worried glance, both realizing the gravity of the situation unfolding in front of them.

Mia cautiously reached towards Alexis, her hands trembling slightly as she checked for signs of life. A soft exhale escaped Mia's lips when she felt a faint pulse under her fingertips. Alexis was alive, but whether the ritual had been a success remained to be seen.

Alexis gasped, air filling her lungs. Sitting up, the the color fully returned to her face.

"I can't... I can't feel it anymore," Alexis said, her eyes wide. "It's gone. The shadow's gone."

"Try activating this sigil," Mia said holding out her arm.

"Which one?" Alexis asked.

"Literally any of them," Mia replied. Alexis reached out and touched one of the simpler markings on Mia's arm. Alexis closed her eyes and silently mouthed a handful of words. It was as sigil designed to light up a room, and took the barest trickle of magic to activate.

Absolutely nothing happened.

Alexis began to tear up, but a smile crossed her lips. "It worked. I'm safe. I can't touch magic, but I'm safe."

"Good," Riley said flatly. "Now let's get the little Lisa ring leader here in there so the murderers can have a happy ending."

"We didn't... I didn't meant to kill Greg," Lisa said quietly, looking at Riley. "I'm never going to feel bad about it because he was a piece of shit who along with his dad blackmailed me to cover up the kid he killed... but that was never our plan, I swear."

"Sure looked like it from the outside," Riley responded.

"If the goal was to just kill him, we could have done a simple fire spell," Alexis responded.

"Or, like, we could have just pushed him in the river while he was drunk," Lisa said, folding her arms. "We just screwed up the ritual we were *actually* trying to do."

"And what was that?" Riley asked.

"I wanted the world to forget him," Lisa said. "I wanted to erase him from the memory of every living thing, so he'd wake up as alone as he made me feel. And he'd be stuck like that forever. No one ever learning his name. No one ever remembering who he was."

"That kind of spell would need the amount of power I felt..." Mia said. "You... you put the sigils too close together didn't you. That's what went wrong. The energy from the spell ended up in a feedback loop and cooked him."

"That's... that's what I think happened?" Alexis said, shaking her head. "I was overconfident when I made the calculations. I should have been more careful."

"This is all good to know, but we're in the middle of a much more urgent situation," Mia said, looking towards Lisa. "We need to get started immediately before—"

The lights began to flicker, and a cold wind seemed to whip through the room.

"Tell me that's just the ghosts," Bobbi said quietly. "Like I'd really like for that to just be the ghosts."

"None of the ghosts are in the room right now," Riley said quietly. "This isn't them."

"Lisa, can you—" Mia started. "Oh shit."

Lisa's eyes were like black voids, and the air seemed to crackle around her. "Help..." Lisa managed to croak out through gritted teeth. "I can't move."

"Alexis, get up," Mia said, her voice filled with urgency. "Bobbi, you and I need to get Lisa into the circle immediately."

"What's happening?" Riley asked, keeping her distance.

"The shadow just saw half its meal disappear," Mia said getting to her feet. "So it's going to try and take what's left on the menu as fast as it can."

"How do we want to do this?" Bobbi asked, approaching Lisa cautiously.

"Grab her left arm and I'll grab her right?" Mia shrugged. "There isn't really a script for this kind of thing?"

Bobbi nodded, steeling herself as she reached out to grab Lisa's left arm. Mia grabbed the right, feeling a surge of dark energy emanating from Lisa as they pulled her towards the circle Mia had hastily drawn on the floor. Lisa's body felt like dead weight, resisting any efforts to move her.

As they reached the edge of the circle, a wave of icy coldness swept through the room, causing the windows to rattle and the walls to groan.

"Hurry!" Mia urged, her voice strained with effort as they dragged Lisa across the threshold of the circle, and pushed her to the ground.

Lisa convulsed, her limbs jerking uncontrollably as she lay within the protective confines of the sigils. Dark tendrils snaked out from her body, reaching towards Mia and Bobbi.

"Mia?" panic filled Bobbi's voice.

"Don't move even if it touches you, keep your hands on the circle. The circle will keep it from attaching to you," Mia instructed. "It's going to hurt… a lot… but I can't spare any energy to stop that right now. The priority's got to be survival and nothing else."

"Got it," Bobbi answered. The dark tendrils snapped at her hands, and the young woman winced in pain. "Fuck that hurts."

"Lisa, if you can hear me, I'm going to sever you from magic now," Mia said, preparing to enact the ritual a second time. "Do I have your permission to do it?"

"Yesh!" Lisa managed to squeeze out.

Mia began the ritual as quickly as she could, rattling off the beginning of the incantation as fast as she could say the words. Power surged through the circle and the sigils scrawled across the floorboards, and Mia did her best to keep her concentration as tendrils of darkness struck at her exposed arms.

Mia just needed to hold on a little longer. To keep pushing as hard as she could, despite the pain she was enduring.

As Mia reached the apex of the ritual, Lisa's body let out a scream, and a torrent of power surged at Mia. She barely had time to reactivate her protection sigils before it tossed her across the room and slammed her into the wall. Her already bruised ribs screamed at her, as she struggled to find footing.

Lisa stood at the center of the circle, her form roiling in darkness.

"I-I thought she wasn't going to fight this," Alexis said, her eyes wide.

"Lisa isn't. The shadow is," Mia responded. "Alexis… we need to keep her in that circle. Bobbi, keep your hands on the sigils. You're the only thing keeping that spell going."

"Not moving an inch," Bobbi replied, looking up at Mia.

Alexis ran to Lisa's side and grabbed her. Lisa's body struggled, and tried to flee — but Alexis held on tight. Tendrils of darkness snapped at Alexis, but they seemed to pass through her, unable to make contact.

"Your little game won't work on her, shadow," Mia smirked as she limped back to the circle. "Alexis has been cut off from all magic, which means you literally can't touch her anymore."

Her body screamed with pain, but Mia knelt down and began the ritual a second time. The shadow's attacks from Lisa's body against her intensified, some breaking skin, other leaving burning welts… but Mia continued through the pain.

A snaking tendril of darkness wrapped around Mia's throat, trying to choke her, to keep her from continuing, but Mia used the last of her protection spell's energy to keep going.

The room filled with an intense energy as Mia chanted the final words of the incantation. She forced herself to keep her eyes on the sigils, her breaths ragged as she poured every last ounce of her strength into the ritual.

As the final words left her lips, the tension in the air seemed to shatter. The entire room rippled with a wave of magic, and Mia could feel the shadow's presence wane. What sounded like thunder cracked in center of the room, shaking the Rose House down to its foundations. In the moments after, the tendrils of darkness retracted from their positions, and Lisa collapsed onto Alexis.

"Lisa!" Bobbi yelled, getting to her feet and helped Alexis guide the young woman's limp form onto the nearby couch.

Lisa's eyes opened wide, and she took a deep breath. The color came back to her face immediately, and she grabbed onto Bobbi.

"I'm sorry I lied to you," Bobbi said quietly.

"I'm sorry I didn't believe you when you tried to tell me the truth," Lisa whispered back.

"Aw, that's sweet," Mia said quietly, the pain from her injuries making it difficult to get up from her hands and knees. "But could someone please drive me to the closest urgent care?"

Chapter 20

"So does it still hurt after a week?" Riley asked, taking a sip of her coffee.

"Oh not really," Mia replied, leaning back in the cafe booth. "Only when I laugh, or cry, or bend over, or turn too quickly, or, y'know, *breathe*..."

"I sometimes get surprised at the lengths you'll go to for relative strangers," Riley sighed, shaking her head. "But I don't know why... you saving me from this kind of thing is how we became friends in the first place."

"If it's in your power to help someone and you don't, then what's the point of anything?" Mia shrugged and then winced. "Also, for the record, *shrugging* hurts."

"I know this is weird, and maybe out of nowhere, but I've been thinking about some of our conversations over the last week," Riley said, shifting in her seat.

"Which one?" Mia said. "We talk a lot, Riley."

"We were last talking about it in my kitchen, right before Lisa and company showed up," Riley replied.

"About how you have way too much peanut butter in your cabinet?" Mia smiled. "Because that's far too much for a normal human person to have."

"First off, it's cheaper to buy in bulk," Riley said. "But no, about right and wrong and..."

"And how you see the world in black and white sometimes? When it's really shades of gray?" Mia responded. "Yeah, I remember. I think you're used to operating in a world where the law treats people fairly, and that people don't have to take matters into their own hands."

"I guess with the magical parts of the world, you can't just call the cops," Riley sighed.

"I mean, I didn't learn that from the 'magical' part of anything though," Mia said, shifting in her seat and trying to get comfortable. "Riley, there are a lot of parts of the mundane world where people can't trust authorities to do anything. Greg Van Buren wasn't the first person to take advantage of a broken system, and he'll be far from the last."

"You're going to have to give me time to get on board with that," Riley said, shaking her head. "Like I see your reasoning, it just doesn't sit right with me still."

"Oh I know in your heart you're an uptight rule follower," Mia winked. "You'll get over it eventually."

"I'm not uptight," Riley pouted.

"You literally wear pantsuits constantly," Mia laughed. "You are the poster girl for uptight."

"How much did that laugh hurt?" Riley said with a smirk.

"Oh so much, but it was worth it," Mia said with a grimace.

"Okay, so I'm a little wound up sometimes," Riley brushed the one stray lock of blonde hair out of her face and tucked it back into place. "But uptight? That's not fair. I know how to let loose."

"Yeah, but I've got to coax it out of you," Mia laughed. "And you're right, 'uptight' might not be the best term. Three drinks deep Riley is a very different person."

"Okay yeah, sometimes I need you to break me out of my shell a bit," Riley replied with a sly smile.

"Then here's to dragging Riley Whittaker out of her shell," Mia said, raising her coffee cup in the air before taking a drink.

"Crap, look at the time," Riley said, standing up. "We should get going, I've got like three classes to teach today."

"Yeah, I've got to open the shop," Mia replied, gently easing herself out of the booth. "Walk me there?"

"Sure, want to take the path through the park by the river?" Riley asked.

Mia paused and just stared at Riley. The look she gave Riley could crack stone.

"Kidding, jeeze, lighten up," Riley said with a grin and her hands up in the air. "We'll take the normal route we'll take the normal route."

The two exited the coffee shop and made their way through the downtown streets of Parrish Mills. A light flurry of snow drifted down lazily from the sky, but was quickly melting when it reached the ground. The roads were a dirty slush of late winter thaw, and each passing car threatened to splash it onto the sidewalk.

"So speaking of what happened, what are we doing with Iggatol's grimoire?" Riley asked as they continued down the road. "We can't just leave that thing sitting around."

"I had Bobbi drop it off at the return slot at the university library," Mia replied with a grimace. "It seems sacrilegious, but it was the easiest way to get it back to them without anyone asking us any awkward questions."

"You had Bobbi put a rare historic one of a kind priceless hand written text… in the library book drop?" Riley's eyes were wide with shock.

"Yup," Mia nodded.

"That is truly insane," Riley laughed.

"Got the job done," Mia smiled.

As they approached the front door of Markov Books, Mia pulled her keys out of her bag and unlocked the front door.

"Honestly, I think I'll just be glad for things to go back to normal for a while," Riley sighed.

"For a while?" Mia asked, raising an eyebrow.

"I mean, yeah," Riley replied. "If there's anything I've learned in the last year and a half there's always going to be another crisis coming. No use worrying about it until it shows up on our doorstep though."

"True," Mia shook her head. "Anyways, we still on for movie night tonight?"

"Absolutely," Riley smiled. "Swing by my place at eight?"

"Great," Mia smiled, stepping into the store. "I'm going to make you watch The Craft."

"We are not watching that!" Riley said, walking off down the street. "We are one hundred percent *not* watching that!"

Mia began turning on the lights to the store, illuminating the shelves filled with with a hodgepodge of crystals, tarot decks, books, and the occasional genuinely useful item. She made her way to the back office, where she began to prep the cash drawer for the register.

Glancing up at the schedule on the wall, things were worse than ever with the number of empty shifts. The store was short staffed already, but things had gotten significantly worse. Alexis was still on the fence about returning to work now that magic was something out of her reach, and Mia couldn't really blame the girl. If she'd been in Alexis's place, being surrounded by constant reminders of what she'd lost might have been too much too.

But it meant that rather than being one worker down, it was two — and Mia was *not* enjoying the overtime.

Mia grabbed a "Help Wanted" sign out of the bottom drawer of her desk, and began to walk up to the front of the store. After putting the drawer in the register, Mia placed the sign in the front window. In some ways she missed the days where she just showed up to work and did what she was told. Being in charge was way less fun.

The larger paycheck was nice though.

The morning went by at its fairly normal pace, just enough early morning customers to justify opening before noon. Mia settled into the quiet almost ritual act of restocking various items around the store, and unpacking the previous night's delivery.

She was only going at about half pace because of the pain in her side, but she was getting the job done.

A quiet day was exactly what she needed right now though. Life in Parrish Mills seemed to go through long periods of stillness punctuated by brief interludes of chaos. It wasn't perfect, but it sure beat her life before. She had good friends and slept in a warm bed every night. It was hard to ask for more than that.

Except for maybe a couple more employees so she didn't have to eat lunch while working.

"So, you're hiring?"

Mia looked up from the box of books she was unloading and made eye contact with Bobbi's smiling face.

"Yeah, why?" Mia smirked. "You looking for a job?"

"Might be?" Bobbi said, now looking a little sheepish. She seemed to blush a little, bringing her pale complexion to a similar shade as her red hair.

"Oh shit, you're serious!" Mia blinked. "Yeah, okay. What is… what kind of work experience do you have?"

"I worked in my dad's store when I was in high school?" Bobbi said quickly. "I know I don't have a lot of witchcraft knowledge but…"

"Bobbi, you've literally fought vampires and faced a true shadow," Mia said, shaking her head. "I'm pretty sure you can handle learning which crystals go where on the shelf. I just didn't know if you'd ever had a job or not."

"I have definitely had a job," Bobbi smiled. "You don't grow up in Gary Crawford's house and not put the work in."

"Can I ask why you want to work here?" Mia asked.

"Well honestly with everything that's happened, I kind of want to know more," Bobbi said, leaning against the counter. "All this supernatural and magical stuff exists whether I understand it or not, and I'd rather be prepared for once."

"Well hell then, you're hired," Mia laughed, and then immediately winced.

"Ooof, still hurting?" Bobbi asked.

"Yeah, doctor said it'll probably be like six weeks?" Mia sighed. "I could probably find some way to speed it up, but sometimes it's best to let this sort of thing fix itself the normal way."

"So I shouldn't stop by for a while," Bobbi winked. "Let you rest and heal?"

"I — uh, I assumed you wouldn't be coming over for *other* reasons?" Mia paused. "First off, if you're going to work here, that's stopping altogether regardless of any other circumstances. I'll be your boss, and that would get incredibly complicated."

"You said first off," Bobbi said. "That implies at least a second thing."

"The second thing is… Lisa?" Mia said. "Like, you're clearly still hung up on her. Like badly. And it's also obvious she likes you too. You're seriously going to let that pass you by?"

"I don't know, Mia," Bobbi looked down. "That entire relationship started on a lie. I don't know how things could recover."

"She also accidentally killed a guy, no one's perfect," Mia replied. "And I know you, Bobbi Crawford. I know you pretty damned well. You like this girl, and you're going to regret it if you don't try."

Bobbi paused, and seemed to contemplate what Mia was saying for a minute.

"But what if… what if I fuck it up," Bobbi said quietly. "It's just so complicated…"

"Then you fuck it up?" Mia answered. "Look, it's the risk you take. But if you just sit on the fence and don't take chances, you end up alone. It's just literally dumb as hell to waste your life pining for someone you could actually be with but are avoiding just because of some baggage."

"Like you and Sarah," Bobbi nodded.

Mia blinked. "Sarah and I were together for almost eleven years. Not like 'me and Sarah' — you dated this girl for like half a week."

Mia playfully threw a pen from the counter at Bobbi, who easily stepped out of the way of the airborne Bic.

"It's a little bit the same," Bobbi smirked.

"No, it's not," Mia said with a smile. "And just for that, you can open the store with me tomorrow, bright and early."

"You're a jerk, Mia Graves," Bobbi smiled.

"Can't call me that, I'm your boss now," Mia replied. "Now go enjoy your last day of unemployed freedom."

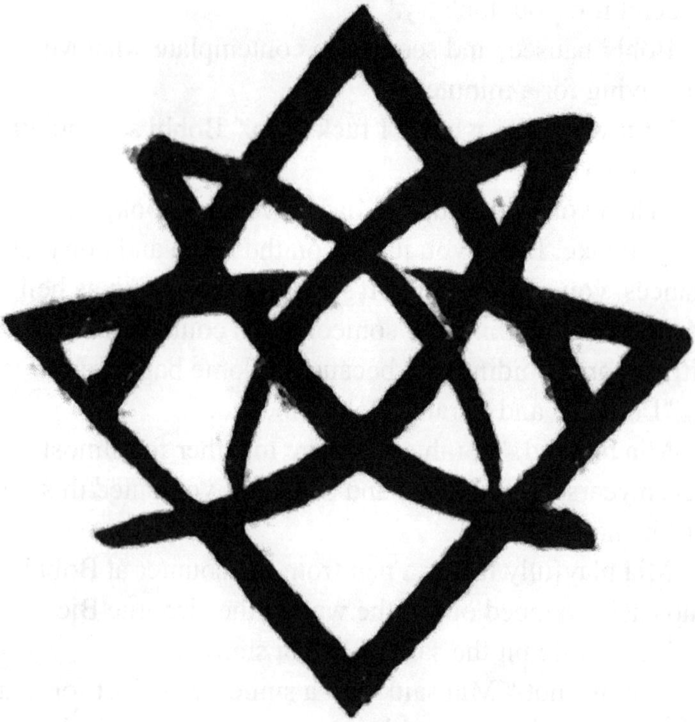

Chapter 21

Bobbi took the long walk back to campus mulling over what Mia had told her. Maybe she was right, and that she needed to take the the risk. Maybe it was worth trying with Lisa.

In all honesty, she'd been avoiding Lisa since the day in the Rose House when they'd severed her from magic. It had been a lot, and Alexis had taken Lisa home. She knew Lisa would be in mourning, with the deaths of Mark and Theresa, and she wanted to give Lisa her space.

But, like, Lisa hadn't actually asked for space?

All of this was based on assumptions Bobbi was making, and she really needed to clarify those things. Making decisions based on how she *assumed* people felt was a great way to screw things up further.

As Bobbi stepped back onto the grounds of Garrity University, she made her way through the hustle and bustle of the busy campus. The buildings cast long shadows in the winter afternoon sun, and Bobbi steeled herself for what was to come.

There were only a handful of places Lisa was likely to be, and Bobbi was willing to go to each one until she found her. Sure, she could call, and sure, she could text. But Bobbi's nerves were curled in the pit of her stomach, and she didn't have the guts to do either of those things.

Bobbi started with the student union. After searching the building for twenty minutes, she couldn't find a single sign of Lisa in her usual spots.

She continued her hunt in the university library, meticulously checking every corner. Bobbi had first met Lisa in the library, before there were any lies between them. They were just two people sharing a moment then.

After a while it was clear Lisa wasn't there either though.

The only place Bobbi knew to check that was left was Lisa's dorm. Bobbi had never been up there, and it was going to make pretending that she was casually running into her impossible.

Bobbi walked towards the dorms, but stopped in the student parking lot that occupied the space between a few of the buildings. Maybe she should give up. Maybe she should just go home. Maybe today wasn't the right time for this.

"Bobbi?"

Bobbi whipped her head around, and saw Lisa standing there, hands thrust in the pockets of her winter jacket.

"Hey," Bobbi said quietly. She had thought up a million things to say to Lisa when she saw her, but all of them just seemed to fall out of her head now that they were finally face to face again.

"I was on my way to go see you," Lisa said, stepping closer. "But here you are."

"How are you... how are you holding up?" Bobbi asked.

"I'm okay," Lisa replied. "We finally got 'missing persons' reports out on Mark and Theresa. They got a footnote in the paper. Didn't even make the front section."

"I'm so sorry about that," Bobbi said nervously. "I know it's not fair."

"I don't know what else I expected," Lisa said with a shrug. "When the son of a wealthy and politically important alumni dies, the university makes a spectacle. When ordinary people do, it just evaporates into the background. It's the way the world is."

"Yeah, but it shouldn't be," Bobbi said, looking Lisa directly in the eye.

"It's okay, I don't care so much about what the rest of the world remembers right now," Lisa said sadly. "I just miss my friends."

Without thinking, Bobbi walked over to Lisa and gave her a hug. Lisa immediately squeezed her back.

"It is freezing out here," Lisa said, still holding on to Bobbi. "Do you want to go inside and keep talking? Like head up to your room or something so we can have some privacy?"

"Yeah, we can do that," Bobbi answered.

The two walked into Bobbi's building and headed up to her room. Lisa walked in and kicked off her boots, sitting down on the edge of Bobbi's futon. "Little different vibe than the last time I was here."

"Yeah, you could say that," Bobbi sighed, leaning against the wall. "I want to be completely honest with you now. I swear, anything you ask me about in this room, I'll give you a straight answer. I know I said it before, but I'm so sorry about lying to you. I didn't mean to…"

"No, I get it," Lisa said, curling up on the futon. "And I probably would have done the same thing in your position. If we'd listened to you and Mia maybe Mark and Theresa wouldn't have died."

"Yeah, but if we'd been straight with you, maybe you would have been more likely to listen to us to begin with," Bobbi replied.

"I mean, you didn't know about Greg, and you didn't know his death was an accident," Lisa said, looking down at the floor. "Like I get being cautious on the approach. It looked like some innocent person got violently murdered. It was a bad situation all around."

Bobbi crossed the room and sat down next to Lisa.

Lisa's eyes were distant as she continued, her voice low and strained. "I just can't shake this feeling of guilt. I was so focused on revenge, on making sure he paid for what he did to me, that I didn't think about the consequences. And now my friends are dead." She paused, her breath shaky, before turning to look at Bobbi. "Do you think there's any way to make things right?"

Bobbi hesitated, unsure of how to respond to such raw vulnerability from Lisa. She could see the pain etched in the lines of Lisa's face, the weight of her choices heavy on her shoulders. Taking a deep breath, Bobbi reached out and gently clasped Lisa's hand in hers.

"Sometimes we can't make things right," Bobbi said softly. "We've just got to be better as we move forward. Like you can't undo the stuff you did wrong, but you can try to do what you can to make sure you don't make the same kind of mistakes in the future… and when you see someone else doing those things, you can stop them."

"I don't know that it makes me feel any better," Lisa said, tucking her feet underneath herself.

"I don't know if anything I say can," Bobbi replied. "But, like… okay. Mia's got this friend Lucy who's a vampire—"

"A what?" Lisa blinked, sitting back up.

"Oh yeah, vampires are real. It's a whole thing," Bobbi said waving her hand. "Anyway, like one or two hundred years ago or something, I don't remember, Lucy did some, like, *super* bad shit. But she was horrified with it, and now she's busy helping keep all the people Dr. Smith turned into vampires in line and not going all evil like she did once."

Lisa stared at Bobbi like she'd grown a second head. "Dr. Smith. Like as in the missing history department head Dr. Carson Smith."

"Oh yeah, he was a vampire. Dude was trying to start an army or a cult or something," Bobbi nodded.

"So you... you know like how he disappeared or something?" Lisa asked, suddenly invested. "What happened to him?"

"Mia's ex-girlfriend Sarah cut his head off?" Bobbi said sheepishly. Bobbi ended up explaining the events of the previous fall in explicit detail to Lisa, who just stared with her eyes wide open.

"Maybe I'm okay not being a witch anymore," Lisa said quietly. "That's like, a *lot*."

"Yeah, the stuff that really scares me is all the demon stuff," Bobbi nodded. "But, like, that stuff's out there whether I know about it or not. I'd rather know so I can be ready for the danger."

"God, we were really like children playing with fire," Lisa sighed, leaning her head against Bobbi's arm. "It's so weird knowing magic is out there and not being able to touch it anymore."

"I'm sorry you had to give it up," Bobbi said quietly. "I know it was important to you."

"At this point, after everything with that shadow thing, I'm much happier to be alive," Lisa said. "I mostly feel sorry for Beeds. She really loved this stuff too. Like she's been obsessed with making spells as efficient as possible. I'm sure she'll be okay, but it's just going to suck for her for a while."

They sat in silence for a moment, Lisa leaning her head against Bobbi's side.

"How much of what happened between us... how much of that was real?" Lisa asked, breaking the silence.

"For me? All of it," Bobbi answered. "I wasn't, like, executing a plan to seduce you or anything. I am frankly not that good of an actress."

Lisa sat up and looked at Bobbi. "I don't know if I'm being stupid right now, or if I'm just reaching out because of grief... but I really like you Bobbi Crawford. I hate how we met, but I'm still glad we did."

"I mean, technically the first time we met in the library I didn't know anything about Greg," Bobbi shrugged. "That entire conversation was one hundred percent just me being awkward talking to a pretty girl."

"You weren't awkward," Lisa smiled. "And you just said I'm pretty."

"Never going to deny that," Bobbi said nervously.

"I know this is a weird time to bring it up, but I'd really like to kiss you right now," Lisa said quietly.

Bobbi felt her heart race at Lisa's words, a mix of emotions swirling inside her. She gazed into Lisa's eyes, seeing the vulnerability and sincerity there. Without a word, she leaned in slowly, closing the distance between them. Their lips met in a tender, hesitant kiss that quickly deepened into something more passionate.

After a few moments their lips parted, and Bobbi found herself staring into Lisa's crystal blue eyes.

"So I have another question," Lisa said, looking up at Bobbi.

"Go ahead," Bobbi replied.

"So... like... Mia and Dr. Whittaker... are they a thing? Like a couple?" Lisa asked. "Because they really act like a couple."

Bobbi started laughing so hard that Lisa had to sit back up. "Oh god no... no no no... oh god..."

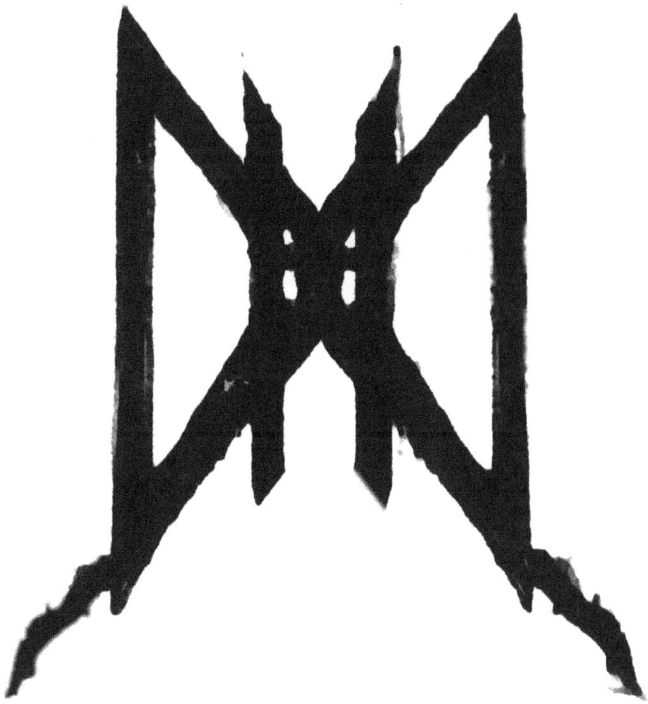

About the Author

Trae Dorn is just your average geeky, nonbinary genderqueer witch. They live just on the edge of the woods somewhere in Wisconsin with their spouse.

They are the creator of the comics UnCONventional and Peregrine Lake. They also run the Nerd & Tie Podcast Network where they host a number of shows including the popular witchcraft podcast BS-Free Witchcraft.

They are also very, very tired.

You can find more about them at **traedorn.com**

Printed in the USA
CPSIA information can be obtained
at www.ICGtesting.com
CBHW051821181124
17605CB00005B/62